CODY'S VARSITY RUSH

BOOK 5

Other Books in the
Spirit of the Game Series

SPIRIT OF THE GAME

CODY'S VARSITY RUSH

BOOK 5

BY TODD HAFER

zonder**kidz**

The children's group of Zondervan

www.zonderkidz.com

Cody's Varsity Rush
Copyright © 2005 by Todd Hafer

Requests for information should be addressed to
Zonderkidz, Grand Rapids, Michigan 49530

Library of Congress Cataloging-in-Publication Data

Hafer, Todd.
    Cody's varsity rush / Todd Hafer.
        p. cm.- (Spirit of the game series ; bk. 5)
    Summary: Now a high school freshman, Cody makes the varsity
football team and struggles with whether to identify himself as a Christian at school and on the playing field.
ISBN-10: 0–310–70794–3 (softcover)
ISBN-13: 978–0–310–70794–3 (softcover)
        [1. Christian life—Fiction. 2. Football—Fiction. 3. Conduct
of life—Fiction. 4. High schools—Fiction 5. Schools—Fiction.]
I. Title.
    PZ7.H11975Cod 2005
    [Fic]–dc22

                                                    2005004292

Cover design by Alan Close
Interior design: Susan Ambs
Art direction: Laura Maitner–Mason
Photos by Synergy Photographic

Printed in the United States of America

05 06 07 08/DCI/5 4 3 2 1

Contents

This book is dedicated to the life and memory of Tim Hanson, a true athlete, a true friend.

Foreword

I love sports. I have always loved sports. I have competed in various sports at various levels right through college. And today, even though my official competitive days are behind me, you can still find me on the golf course working on my game, or on a basketball court playing a game of pick-up.

Sports have also helped me learn some of life's important lessons—lessons about humility, risk, dedication, teamwork, friendship. Cody Martin, the central character in "The Spirit of the Game" series, learns these lessons too. Some of them the hard way. I think you'll enjoy following Cody in his athletic endeavors.

Like most of us, he doesn't win every game or every race. He's not the best athlete in his school, not by a long shot. But he does taste victory, because, as you'll see, he comes to understand that life's greatest victories aren't reflected on a scoreboard. They are the times when you rely on a strength beyond your own—a spiritual strength—to carry you through. They are the times when you put the needs of someone else before your own. They are the times when sports become a way to celebrate the life God has given you.

So read on, and may you always possess the true Spirit of the Game.

Toby McKeehan

Chapter 1
Back in the Danger Zone

Cody strained against the weight on his chest. He hungered for one more bench press, but now the bar seemed rooted to his torso.

"A little help," he gasped. He wondered if his plea was loud enough for anyone in the Grant High School weight room to hear. A few seconds passed. He wondered if anyone had died this way—pinned to a weight bench and slowly crushed by 135 pounds of iron.

He felt relief wash over him when the Evans twins, Bart and Brett, appeared on either side of the bench. They each grabbed one end of the long iron bar and lifted it from Cody's chest, helping him extend his arms and replace it atop the posts that rose like crossbars at the head of the bench.

"Thanks for the spot, guys," Cody said. "I shoulda stopped at three reps."

"No problem, Martin," Bart said. "Doing reps with 135? That's pretty good. That's five pounds better than my max." He looked down at Cody. "It looks like you're starting to get some guns on you. Robyn Hart's gonna be impressed."

"Squirt guns, maybe," Cody said, ignoring the dig. "Some of the juniors and seniors are lifting twice what I'm doing." He sat up and looked around the room. At this early hour, 8:00 a.m., it was mostly frosh and sophomore football hopefuls trying to prepare for the upcoming season. The older players would arrive a bit later. Cody wanted to finish his workout before that happened. It was embarrassing to watch guys warm up with the kind of weight that he could lift only a few times—and then only with much grunting and ungainly effort.

"Hey," Bart said, dislodging Cody from his thoughts. "Chop's here!"

Cody turned to the entrance expecting to see Pork Chop Porter smiling, flexing his thick arms, and telling everyone, "Okay, time to load up all bars and machines with the man-weights. Chop's in the house!"

But Chop stood in the doorway somber and quiet, his eyes scanning the room. When he locked on Cody, he raised his right arm and made a curling motion with his forefinger.

Cody frowned and followed Chop out of the weight room.

"What's up, Chop?" he asked once they were outside, squinting against the bright late-August sun. You look like your breakfast didn't agree with you or something."

Chop didn't appear to have heard him. "Dude, Gabe Weitz is back in town," he said grimly.

"Gabe Weitz?" Cody was surprised by the shrillness of his own voice. "That psycho loser? I thought he got thrown in jail up in Denver earlier in the summer. Assault charges."

"Yeah, that's what I heard too," said a voice behind Cody.

Cody turned 180 degrees to face Bart, who had followed him out the door.

Pork Chop wagged his head slowly. "I don't know where he was, dawgs; I just know he's back. I was in Dairy Delight last night—I just stopped in for a chocolate shake to go—and he walks in. He comes over to me, and I think he's gonna take a swing at me. But he just says, 'Hello, Porter. You doin' okay? And how about your little friend?'"

"Whoa!" Bart said. "What did you say to him?"

"I didn't say anything. I just stared at him. Tried to stare right through him. And I made sure I held my ground. He was right up in my face, but there was no way I was takin' a step back. Finally, he walks away and goes up to the counter, probably to see if the Double D has a Loser Meal or something. So, I figure I can go now, right? I get to the door and I hear him say, 'See you guys around.' I don't like the way he said it. It was a threat, no doubt."

Cody groaned. "Man, I thought we were done with that guy."

Bart scrunched up his forehead. "What does he have against you guys anyway? I mean, this isn't still about your brother laying the smackdown on him last winter, is it, Chop?"

Pork Chop sighed heavily. "I think it is, at least partially. He wanted revenge big-time after that. He tried to hit us with beer bottles one time. Then he went after Co and Drew Phelps during track season. Chased 'em all over town."

"Crazy," Bart said. "When's he gonna give up?"

"Probably not till one of us is in the hospital," Pork Chop answered. "Or the morgue."

The words made Cody shudder. He recalled how easily Weitz had thrown him against the Grant Middle School gym door and then had tossed him, like a rag doll, in a snowbank. All for the heinous crime of letting the door close and lock behind him.

Cody pictured how Pork Chop had come to his rescue before Weitz could pull him out of the snow and pummel him some more. Chop had held his own against the larger, older enemy.

Then Doug Porter had appeared. One vicious uppercut to the stomach and it was over. Weitz's ab muscles—if he had any muscles under his substantial beer gut—were probably still aching now, almost a year later.

"Look guys," Bart said, apparently uncomfortable with the uneasy silence, "so what if he's back. I mean, if he messes with either one of you, you just call Doug, right, Chop? And he comes down from Boulder and stomps a mud hole in Weitz, once and for all."

Pork Chop chewed thoughtfully on his bottom lip. "That's not gonna happen, dawg. Doug's a college football player now. And you know what's been happenin' in college ball lately. The scandals and stuff. That 'boys will be boys' junk—it's so over now. Doug's gotta keep his nose clean or he gets booted off the team. It's as simple as that. Besides, Boulder's a long way from Grant, and I don't even think he's comin' home till Thanksgiving. Maybe during a bye week in mid-October. That's almost two months away. Co and I could be dead meat by then."

"So what are you going to do?" Bart asked, his voice becoming nasal and whiney.

Pork Chop looked at Cody. "Try to stay alive. Watch each other's backs, right, dawg?"

Cody nodded. "Just like always."

Pork Chop forced a smile. "Well that's enough of that subject. Time to go throw some iron around. Yet one more reason to get all swole now."

"You already look pretty swole to me," Bart said, his voice full of admiration. "I mean, you get bigger every time I see you. What's your secret?"

Pork Chop eyed his teammate suspiciously, then snorted. "No secret. Just hard work."

"Yeah," Cody said. "Nobody puts in the work like Chop. He'll work all day helping his dad on the farm and *then* go hit the weight room."

Bart whistled through his teeth. "Well, Chop, it's workin'—big time!"

Chop smiled broadly. "What can I say? I'm a man of steel and sex appeal. But don't worry, Co, I won't try to steal Ms. Hart from you."

Cody shook his head. "Great. First Bart and now you bustin' my chops about that. I can see some things aren't gonna change from eighth grade. Can you both repeat after me: 'Cody Martin and Robyn Hart are NOT boyfriend/girlfriend. Period.'"

Pork Chop frowned. "Could you run through that one more time, dawg? I think I missed part of it."

"Yeah, me too," Bart chimed in.

Cody tried to load his voice with as much disgust as he could muster. "Whatever. Come on. Let's go throw some weights around. The first official practice is only three days away."

Cody swallowed hard and whispered, "Know how those sportscasters are always talking about somebody being 'a man among boys?' I feel like one of those boys right now. You know how hard we worked this summer, but my arms look like garter snakes—in a room full of pythons!"

"Yeah," said Pork Chop, without turning around. "Some of these dudes make *me* look small. I'm not used to that."

Cody surveyed the scene. It was the first day of football practice, and the locker room buzzed with activity. The older players, seniors and juniors, already had their equipment and were dressing out in front of their freshly painted deep-blue lockers.

Cody drew in a deep breath and let it escape as a low whistle. Several of the hulking linemen had tattoos. His dad would be freaking out if he were here. He put tattoos and body piercing in the same category: senseless self-mutilation.

Cody wondered what Brendan Clark would say about that characterization. The all-state middle linebacker sported a double-strand barbed wire design around the bulge of his right bicep. On his left shoulder was the full-color trademark *S* of Superman.

A coiled cobra, fangs bared and dripping droplets of venom, stared menacingly from the midback of senior Jeff "Truck" Tucker, a six two, 230-pound defensive end who had amassed eighty-five tackles, nineteen sacks, and ten knocked-down passes the previous season. Pork Chop knew all of the key Grant High defensive stats. He could recite them to Cody as easily as he could recite the multiplication table up to twelve.

"ATV!" Cody heard Clark bellow. He turned his attention to the linebacker again. Clark was exchanging fist pounds with Gordon Daniels, nicknamed ATV, for all-terrain vehicle. Daniels had the powerful, compact build of a pit bull. He would start at fullback now that Doug Porter, Pork Chop's all-world brother, had graduated. If not for Doug, ATV would have probably been a starter since his freshman year. Every football player at Grant Middle School had known about ATV. Only five ten, but 210 solid pounds. He could bench-press 340 pounds, squat 525, and run the forty-yard dash in 4.7 seconds.

"Dude," Cody said, "ATV's beard stubble is almost as thick as my dad's."

Pork Chop, still not turning around, offered, "Yeah, it's almost as thick as my Aunt Wanda's."

Cody chuckled softly, not wanting to risk some senior asking, "Hey, freshman, what's so funny, stick-figure boy?" Cody looked down at his arms and shoulders. He knew he should have hit the weights harder over the summer, but baseball had gobbled up too much time. Then there were the morning runs with Drew Phelps, helping his friend prepare for cross-country season. *I'm in decent shape*, he thought, *but looking at these guys, I have a feeling that "decent" isn't going to cut it in high school football. I wish I could have made it to preseason football camp, but I couldn't leave the guys on the baseball team hangin'.*

At least, he reassured himself, *I don't have to play against these bigger, older guys. I'm not like Chop. I'm not gonna make varsity. And that's a good thing. These monsters would kill me. All I want to do is play freshman ball—maybe get called up to JV by the end of the season.*

Cody trained his eyes on the bronze back of his best friend. His shoulders were thicker and broader than ever. Chop was getting taller all the time too. "Growing faster than the national debt," as Mr. Porter said.

Everyone would know just how tall Chop was in a few moments, when the two of them got to the front of the line where Mr. Curtis, an assistant coach, and Larry Vance, the team manager were busy weighing and measuring.

Bart Evans, who had quarterbacked the Grant Middle School teams, was on the scale now. Curtis adjusted a thin metal arm that was attached to the scale, sliding it up, then unfolding a foot-long piece that jutted out from the arm at a ninety-degree angle, and resting it atop Bart's closely shorn brown hair. Cody had seen the same kind of scale in the doctor's office.

"Evans, Bart," Curtis called out in a nasal monotone voice. "Height: Five feet eleven inches. Weight: A buck sixty."

Vance, who reminded Cody of the singer Steven Curtis Chapman, sat in a metal folding chair next to the scale, a computer not much bigger than Cody's Bible perched on his lap. The manager's fingers danced across the keyboard logging Bart's information.

It was Chop's turn now. He waited for Curtis to nod, then hopped on the scale with both feet.

"Easy there, young Mr. Porter," Curtis warned, but his voice was still as flat as the voice that announced the time and temperature on the phone. "This is sensitive equipment here."

Cody noted that many of the upperclass players had stopped joking and swapping stories to study Chop. Even Clark was watching carefully. *Guess this is what it's like when you're the little brother of a legend,* Cody reasoned.

"Porter, Deke," Curtis was saying, raising his voice for the benefit of the intrigued onlookers. "Six feet even, 215 pounds."

That brought a few hoots and whistles. Two-hundred-plus-pound freshmen didn't come along every day, especially when the weight was mostly muscle.

"Chop's almost as thick as his bro," ATV called out.

"Yeah, but can he play like DP?" someone asked.

Cody half expected Chop to turn and flex his thick arms for his teammates, but his friend stepped off the scale softly, nodded at Cody, and went to get fitted for pads and a helmet.

Cody stared at the digital readout at the bottom of the scale, which flashed only a series of dashes after Curtis reset it. He hoped he'd put on at least some muscle since last football season, when he'd weighed in at 120. He remembered Chop's words as they'd bench-pressed in the high school weight room a few days previously—"Dawg, you gotta get more junk in your trunk if you wanna play ball with the big boys. A buck twenty ain't gonna cut it. I bet some of the high school cheerleaders weigh more than that!"

"Martin, Cody." The words snapped Cody back to the present. "Let's see what we got here," Curtis said. "Five feet ten, 140 pounds."

Cody sighed hopefully. *Well*, he thought, *at least my trunk's a little junkier. And maybe I can put on a few more pounds during the season. It would be nice to get up to a buck fifty.*

From the locker room, Cody and the other first-year players filed like cattle to the gym, where stations were set up to fit them with pads and helmets.

Brett Evans, Bart's wide receiver brother, caught up to Cody at the helmet station. "Code," he said, "do you think this is how the knights of old did things? Move from station to station, getting their coats of mail, helmets, armor, swords, and shields?"

Cody chuckled. "I don't know, Brett. I guess I never thought of that. But, hey, we are kind of like knights. The equipment is kinda the same, and Chop always says that high school football is a battle."

Brett swallowed. "Yeah, a battle against bigger, stronger, faster guys than we ever faced back in middle school."

"Meaner, too. Don't forget meaner. Chop says that a couple of teams have these 'pain pools,' where you get money if you put somebody out of a game."

"For real? I don't think that kind of thing would be allowed."

Cody shook his head in disbelief. "I didn't say it was legal. I'm just saying that Chop says it happens."

"If that's true," said Bart, joining the duo, "I hope I *never* play varsity."

Brett rolled his eyes. "Aw, c'mon, bro. This is the big time. This is high school football. We've waited for this for a long time. Besides, I'm sure that pain pool stuff is just urban legend. Right, Cody?"

"I hope so," Cody answered solemnly. "If that kinda stuff goes on, I'm joining the choir."

"I don't know about that," Brett said. "I've heard you sing!"

Cody chuckled and pulled on a helmet. A high school helmet. He thought of all the Grant High games he'd seen from the stands as a grade-schooler, then a middle-schooler. During the early-season contests you could work on your tan while you enjoyed the action on the field.

When late October rolled around and the Colorado temperatures nose-dived, Cody, his mom, and Pork Chop had sat in puffy down coats, hunched together for warmth. Cody's mom always brought a thermos the size of a cheese log, filled with homemade hot chocolate that was typically gone before halftime. Cody's dad rarely came to the games, and when he did, he complained about the "blistering sun" or the "arctic temperatures," depending on the weather. And he complained about the "rock-hard bleachers" *all* the time.

When Cody and Pork Chop entered middle school, they began to count down the years until they would wear the blue and silver of the Grant High Eagles. While watching their first game as sixth graders, Pork Chop shook half a box of Hot Tamales into his mouth and told Mrs. Martin, "You better enjoy our company while you can, Mrs. M, because in just a coupla years Co and I won't be able to sit with you anymore. We'll be out there on the field, tearing it up!"

"I'll be here regardless." She smiled. "Screaming my fool head off for you both. And when it gets cold, I guess I'll be drinking all the hot chocolate myself. Unless Luke starts coming with me."

Pork Chop frowned. "Well, maybe you can smuggle me a cup of cocoa down to the bench, you know. I can tell the coaches it's Gatorade. I mean, I don't know what you do to your cocoa, but it is *sick*!"

Cody's mom looked hurt for a moment. Cody put

his hand on her shoulder. "It's okay, Mom, sick is a good thing."

She arched her eyebrows. "Sick? A good thing?"

Cody and Pork Chop nodded in unison.

Cody's mom sniffed. "I weep for today's youth," she said, winking at them.

Cody and Pork Chop's sixth-grade year was the same season that Doug Porter began writing his legend as Grant's most celebrated athlete. "DP," as Chop called him, showed up at preseason football camp with a shaved head, 220 pounds of muscle, and a sub-five-second forty-yard-dash time, placing him among the fastest gridders in the freshman class. Most important, DP brought a work ethic that put many of the junior and senior players to shame.

He won the starting fullback job early in the season and spent Friday nights and Saturday afternoons running over—and, once in a while, around—Eagle opponents. Midway in the season, teammates began calling him Rhino, for his angry, hard-charging style.

On defense, Rhino Porter played middle guard. By late season, he was known as one of the fiercest hitters in the state. Many opposing teams turned to a steady diet of end runs and out patterns to avoid the middle of the field, which was Rhino's turf.

Whenever the elder Porter charged up the middle for a long touchdown run, or body slammed a quarterback to the ground, Pork Chop would stand and bow to the crowd, boasting, "That's my big bro—taught him everything he knows!"

Pork Chop's proclamations would draw curious looks from newcomers to Eagle football, who would stare at Chop's caramel skin, then turn their eyes to the sidelines, as Rhino removed his helmet and steam rose like smoke from the ghostly white skin of his shaved head.

Cody knew that Chop loved confusing newbies, as he called them. The people who didn't know that Doug was the only child from Tom Porter's first marriage, which had ended in divorce. Doug was only two when his dad met Richelle Taylor at a Denver Broncos game. She moved from big-city South Denver to the small-town farm country of Grant eighteen months later. Pork Chop arrived ten months after the wedding. He was barely out of diapers when his mother declared Grant "too small and too white—if you get my meaning" and separated from her husband. They divorced before Chop started preschool.

Cody grinned as he saw Pork Chop holding his helmet in both hands as if it were the Hope Diamond. The blue plastic crown was well polished and reflected the gym's lights. It reminded Cody of a brand-new bowling ball.

Chop's voice was quiet, reflective. "Just feel this, dawg. Feel the weight. This is a *man's* helmet. It's beautiful. It'll almost hurt me to get it all bashed and battered and stuff."

"You sure you can bust up these helmets, Chop?" Cody asked, turning his own headgear around in his hands like a piece of prize fruit. "These feel real solid. Better made than the ones we had last year."

Pork Chop slapped himself across his barrel chest. "Last year was eighth grade," he said. "This is no eighth-grade body. Hey, Singletary broke sixteen helmets in college. That's intensity, my brother. That's fierce. That's what I'm gonna bring. Every game. Every practice too."

Cody nodded. He frowned as he watched Chop's expression change. The bravado drained from his face. "I wonder," he said quietly, "if my mom will come down for any games. And I wish your mom was here to watch our high school careers."

"Me too," Cody half whispered.

"But she's up there watching, right?" Chop said, stabbing a blunt forefinger into the sky. "Best seat in the house, right?"

"I guess so," Cody said, feeling the familiar pain return. It sat like a brick in his stomach.

Chapter 2

Brendan Clark in the Dark

Lydell!" Cody heard the bear growl of Coach Alvin's voice. Coach Alvin coached receivers and offensive and defensive backs and was as manic as head coach Martin Morgan was quiet and calm. "That stunk, son. Phillips turned you inside out. You have got to move your feet!"

Cody looked up from the soccer field where the freshmen were practicing, to the "official" practice field where the varsity was going at it in the first full-on scrimmage before the season opener. "Man," he mumbled to himself, "I'm glad I'm not Winston Lydell. Coach A has been yapping at him all afternoon. I couldn't take it."

Brett, who was stretching near Cody, heard the comments. "Yeah, I'm sure glad we're freshman cornerbacks, not varsity ones like Lydell."

Cody nodded. "I wonder why Coach is riding Lydell so hard. I mean, he's really pretty good."

"Well, Lydell is gonna be a target this season. I think that's why. There are a lot of good QBs in the conference this year, and there's no way they are gonna throw at Craig Ward. I mean, he's probably the best cover guy in the state. So guess who's gonna get tons of balls thrown his way?"

Cody nodded again. "Yeah, that makes sense. Dude, I wouldn't want that kind of pressure."

Brett snorted. "Tell me about it. If you're a lineman and you miss a tackle, maybe no one will notice, with all the bodies flying around. Besides, maybe a linebacker will have your back and make the play. But if you're a corner and a wideout makes toast out of you in a fly pattern for a TD, the whole world knows."

Cody groaned. "Don't remind me. Makes me want to be a punter."

<hr />

Paul Vance, Larry's brother, was a former Grant center who was built like a fire hydrant. He coached the freshman football team, along with Chris Hendricks, a student teacher and volunteer assistant. After two weeks of practice, Cody decided he liked both of them. Coach Vance was louder than Mr. Smith, the eighth-grade coach, but not as sarcastic. He lacked Smith's mean streak.

As for Hendricks, he smiled whenever anyone called him "Coach," and Cody liked it that he referred to everyone by his first name rather than last name. Coach Hendricks was a first-class jock, too. He had been an all-state defensive back in Kansas and played two years of small-college ball.

Whenever Coach Hendricks spoke, Cody tried to memorize every word. He also appreciated how the young coach took the time to demonstrate footwork and tackling techniques.

Midway through week three of practice, the Grant Middle School eighth graders trotted next door to the high school practice field for the annual eighth grade versus freshmen scrimmage. Before kickoff, Cody chuckled as he saw a small cluster of middle schoolers across the field eyeing their larger opponents, pointing and shaking their heads. One of the group was Pat Hart, Robyn's younger brother. He was the team's quarterback—a high-energy player who always made things happen. But not always good things.

While Coaches Smith and Vance talked at midfield, Cody trotted across to Hart and his teammates.

"Pat," he said cheerfully, "you and your posse can relax. Chop's not scrimmaging today. He's already made varsity. Looks like he'll start on the O-line."

"Thank God," Pat said. From the sincerity in his voice, Cody could tell young Hart meant the expression literally. He clapped Pat on his left shoulder pad. "Have a good scrimmage, Hart. Take it easy on us, okay?"

Pat smiled. It reminded Cody of Robyn's smile.

The middle schoolers received the opening kickoff and returned it to their own thirty-six. Cody felt his hands tingling as he lined up against a tiny wide receiver with an ill-fitting practice jersey. The first play was a handoff to the fullback up the middle. He was swarmed at the line of scrimmage, and the mini receiver didn't even have time to get to Cody and throw a block. He didn't look as if he wanted to.

On the second play, Pat tried a sneak up the middle and gained half a yard. Again, Cody's opponent pulled up before contact. *Come on*, he thought, *somebody please bring some game my way. I'd at least like to get my uniform dirty.*

On third down, Cody watched the little wideout eying his QB. The QB called out the snap count, trying to make his voice deeper than it was.

Aw, you didn't even glance at Mr. Hart the first two plays, little man, Cody thought. *So I bet this ball's coming to you.*

The center snapped the ball, and Pat dropped back into pass formation. The receiver charged at Cody, faked to the inside of the field, then cut for the sideline. Cody followed him like a shadow, risking a quick glance into the backfield.

Pat released the ball as soon as his receiver made his cut. The ball fluttered and wobbled toward its target like an overweight duck trying to fly. *Dude*, Cody thought, *I think Robyn has a better arm than you.*

For a moment, the ball seemed to hang in midair, as if levitated by a magician. *All mine*, Cody thought. He darted to the ball and made sure he secured it in both hands before dashing for the end zone. Looking downfield, he saw Pat angling toward him. The QB made a game effort to cut him off, but, as Cody surmised as he whipped by his would-be tackler, Robyn must have gotten all the speed in the Hart family— along with the arm strength.

Brett arrived in the end zone only a few seconds after Cody. The two banged helmets. "Way to break on that ball," the other corner gushed. "You really sniffed that one out."

Cody laughed dismissively. "Well, it wasn't that hard. That little wideout might as well have told me the play. He totally telegraphed it."

The middle schoolers went three and out on their next possession, and Marcus Berringer, a hard-running halfback, scored on a sixty-eight-yard sweep around the right end on the freshmen's first offensive play.

Midway through the second quarter, the score was 28–0, with the freshmen driving again. Pat Hart had engineered one drive deep into opposition territory, but the mini receiver, working against one of Cody's backups at corner, dropped a perfect pass as he ran into the end zone.

The coaches met at midfield again, both nodding like bobble-head dolls. They shook hands, and Vance turned and jogged to the sideline. "The scrimmage is over," he announced. "No need to continue the carnage."

Cody dipped his head. He already had two pass deflections and three solo tackles to go with the interception and return for a TD. "Man," he muttered to Brett, who was standing next to him. "I know I could get another pick. Poor Pat Hart has no zip on his passes today."

"Yeah," Brett said. "And did you see how my bro was shredding their secondary? He was having fun!"

Friday night brought the varsity season opener at Grant's home field. Cody and his frosh teammates filled the first two rows of aluminum bleachers, eager to cheer on their team, especially Pork Chop and Marcus, who suited up as a third-team tailback.

Grant High School sat on a ridge just above the football field, and before each game, the Eagles would burst from the locker room and thunder down a well-worn path to the field. At the bottom of the path, cheerleaders clutched a circular metal frame that held a construction-paper sign crafted by the Pep Club. Tonight's sign urged "SMASH THE SAINTS," in honor of the visiting team from Holy Family. Accompanying the message was a drawing of a muscle-bound Eagle clasping a sledgehammer in its right talon.

Clark was the first player to pop through the sign, drawing a roar from the crowd. Others followed, clawing for remaining scraps of the tattered sign as they charged through the hoop.

Clark lined up the team for warm-ups, his voice a rumbling baritone that Cody struggled to believe could be generated by a seventeen-year-old's vocal cords.

Grant was the heavy favorite. Cody studied the opposition warming up at the south end of the field and counted only twenty-eight Saints. That meant a lot of guys would have to play offense and defense.

Grant head coach Martin Morgan carried forty-one athletes on his varsity roster, and that was after cutting five seniors that he deemed not up to playing varsity ball. Some coaches let seniors play JV, but Coach Morgan didn't believe in robbing practice and game time from younger players—players who might earn their way up to varsity someday.

The Saints won the pregame coin toss and elected to receive the opening kickoff. "Receive" was a bit of a misnomer when it came to ATV's kickoffs. Cody tried to remember one of the powerful athlete's kicks that had actually been returned.

ATV charged toward the ball, which rested on the kickoff tee almost perfectly perpendicular to the field. As he made contact, the ball seemed to explode off his right foot. Cody watched in awe as it flew in tight, end-over-end somersaults through the uprights, bounced once, then hopped over the chain-link fence that marked the outer boundary of Grant Field.

Last year, Cody had seen one of ATV's kickoffs, aided by a powerful tail wind, clear that fence on the fly, landing in the bed of a Ford pickup parked on the road south of the field. Still, this most recent kick wasn't bad for an early-season effort.

Holy Family showed desperation early, trying a gadget play on first down. Minnery, the Saint QB, handed off to his fullback, who then flipped the ball right back. "Pass! Pass!" Cody heard the coaches screaming on the sideline.

Yancey Mack, the Saints' star wideout, sprinted down the center of the field. Lydell trailed him by two strides. *Uh-oh*, Cody thought, *Lydell must have bit on the fake. This is trouble.*

Cody knew Yancey Mack. Cody had competed against Yancey's little brother in middle school. Both of the Macks were fine athletes. Minnery lofted a high, tight spiral. Cody held his breath.

"Dude," Bart said, "if Mack catches it, he's takin' it all the way to the house. Look—Winston can't keep up with him."

Cody nodded.

The pass looked a bit short. Looking back for it, Mack slowed his pace and extended his arms back for the ball.

Come on, Cody urged silently, *here's your chance, Lydell, close on him. Now!*

The underthrown pass did give the Grant corner time to catch up with Mack. The two were side by side as the Saint receiver pulled the ball into his chest. But then, with the ball secured, Mack went into sprint mode again.

Lydell was candy.

"Aw, man," Bart groaned. "Mack's leaving Winston Lydell behind like he's a stationary object! Coach is gonna have him running gassers all week!"

Grant quickly answered the Saint score. ATV tripped over one of his own blockers on first down, gaining five yards to the Eagle thirty. The next play sent ATV off left tackle. Pork Chop was left tackle. Chop backed his opponent up five steps and sealed him to the inside of the field. ATV charged through the gaping hole. He bowled over a linebacker at the thirty-eight and chugged through yards and yards of open field before dragging a cornerback and a free safety into the end zone.

A pack of grade-school students, aware of ATV's kicking prowess, stood outside the field area in the middle of the road at the field's north end, awaiting the extra point. ATV kicked the ball over all of their heads, sending them scrambling into the parking lot to find it.

ATV's ensuing kickoff bounced off the crossbar in the Saint end zone, giving Holy Family a first down at its own twenty.

After a quarterback draw picked up six yards on first down, the Saints lined up in shotgun formation, with Minnery standing three steps behind his center. As Minnery bellowed the snap count, Mack went in motion, jogging toward Craig Ward's side of the field.

"Check this," Brett said, his puberty-stricken voice cracking, "Mack's gonna go up against Ward? That's crazy! Ward will be on him like a second skin."

On the snap of the ball, Mack bolted into the Grant secondary. He ran up to Ward as if he were meeting a long-lost brother, than planted his left foot and turned 180 degrees back toward his quarterback. Ward stayed right behind him, ready to tackle him as soon as the ball arrived.

But Mack had no intention of gaining only a few yards. He did another 180 and dashed toward the end zone.

A hook-and-go, Cody thought. *Man, Mack runs a crisp pattern. And that was a pretty good pump fake Minnery just gave.*

Ward must have found the pattern crisp too, or maybe he bit on the pump fake. Whatever the case, he overplayed his opponent. When Mack turned and went long, he left Ward behind. Minnery reared back and launched the long ball. It looked to Cody like he put everything into the pass, not wanting to under-throw to his ace receiver again.

"This is bad, this is bad, this is bad," Bart chanted.

Mack was running under the ball now. It looked as if he would be able to catch it in stride. Ward had recovered, but he still lagged two strides behind. Mack looked over his left shoulder. Cody heard one of the two athletes grunt from the supreme effort he was exerting, but he wasn't sure which one.

The ball descended toward Mack's eager hands as he crossed the twenty-five-yard line. Ward, closing on Mack's left side, leaped into the air.

Cody heard a stew of gasps and shouts of "Noooooo!" behind him in the bleachers.

Cody had seen Craig Ward dunk a basketball with two hands, but some guys didn't have the same hops when pack-muling a dozen or so pounds of football padding.

Ward wasn't one of those guys. Sailing upward, he deftly batted the football away from Mack, and the receiver trotted toward the end zone holding nothing but unfulfilled expectations.

"Did you see that?" Cody shouted, grabbing Bart by his freshman game jersey. "That was big-time closing speed! That was big-time hops!"

"Yeah," Brett said admiringly. "No wonder they call Ward's side of the field the No Passing Zone. That's a DB who can handle his business, just like us this year, right, Cody?"

Cody laughed dismissively. "Yeah, whatever," he said.

Yeah, I hope so, he thought.

Ward's big defensive play turned the momentum of the game. Grant went ahead by two touchdowns before halftime, and in the second half, Brendan Clark took over the game. Early in the third quarter he sacked Minnery in his own end zone for a safety. Two series later, he collapsed the pocket, forcing a bad pass that Ward intercepted and returned for a touchdown.

Midway through the fourth quarter, Clark bull-dozed a Saint halfback behind the line of scrimmage, forcing a fumble that was pounced on by ATV. With the score 30–7, Coach Morgan sent in his second team. The backup unit earned two first downs before punting the ball away.

Lydell was flagged for pass interference on third-and-long, which allowed the Saints to get in field goal range and make the final score a slightly more respectable 30–10.

The third-team offense, sparked by Berringer, was driving for a possible late score when time expired. Before he joined his teammates in their stampede to the locker room, Pork Chop detoured toward the bleachers. Before Cody and the Evanses could congratulate him, he shouted, straining to be heard above the buzzing, euphoric crowd, "Code, did you see Weitz around tonight? The bleachers? The snack bar? Anywhere?"

Cody shook his head. "Nah, dude. No sign of him. Go enjoy this. This is really cool. And you played a fierce game. Didn't allow a single sack."

Pork Chop dipped his head. "Thanks, dawg. Hey, you guys gotta come join the celebration. After all, you're Eagles too."

The Grant locker room was bedlam. ATV worked the room like a party host, moving from locker to locker and exchanging high fives and fist pounds with every teammate.

When ATV arrived at Pork Chop's locker, he clasped both hands around his face, like a vise. "That's the way to hold it down on the O-line, big Chop. I could have driven my truck through those holes you were blasting. And I have a big truck! Your big brother woulda been proud if he could have seen you tonight!"

Pork Chop stood—speechless—something Cody didn't witness very often. Chop could manage only a grateful nod.

When ATV finished his rounds he threw back his head and released a howl that reverberated off the concrete floor, steel lockers, and cinder-block walls. Then he punctuated his victory cry by flushing three urinals in quick succession.

"We should go congratulate ATV," Bart said to Cody and Brett. They were watching the celebration from just inside the entrance.

"Yeah," Cody agreed.

The trio approached ATV, who had shucked his jersey and shoulder pads. Cody noted that his sweat-soaked gray T-shirt bore the hand-scrawled message across the chest: "100%—Every Play!"

"Great game, ATV!" Brett said. Cody and Bart nodded their agreement.

"Hey, thanks, freshmen!" ATV boomed. "You see how it's done? You see how good it feels to win? Take note. That's gonna be you out there someday!"

"Another hundred-yard game for you, huh?" Cody offered.

"One hundred and forty-six—in only three quarters! That's 12.9 yards per carry. But who's counting?"

"That's awesome," Cody said, smiling. "Hey, do you know where Clark is? He had twenty solo tackles. We counted. We wanna tell him."

ATV rolled his eyes and tilted his head in the direction of the wrestling room. "He's in his chapel, just like always."

There was something in ATV's voice when he said "just like always." Cody couldn't tell if it was disgust or bewilderment.

"Chapel?" Brett said. "I don't get it."

"Go see for yourself," ATV said with a shrug.

The team was singing the Eagle fight song, off-key and at full volume, when Cody and the Evans brothers headed for the wrestling room only a few steps from the locker room doors.

The wrestling room's double wooden doors creaked softly when Cody and Brett pushed them open. The lights were off. The only illumination came from the moonlight that filtered through a row of windows along one side of the low-ceilinged rectangular room.

Brendan Clark was in a far corner, on his knees, moonlight gathered around him. The scene reminded Cody of a movie, but he couldn't recall which one. He could see Clark's lips moving, but he heard no sound.

Bart started to say something, but Cody poked an elbow in his side and held a forefinger to his lips. Bart shrugged, confused, but after a few seconds, nodded in apparent understanding.

After a minute or so passed, Clark popped to his feet. He walked toward the trio, narrowing his eyes. "Cody Martin and the Evans twins, right?" he asked.

The three looked at each other stunned. Cody knew he and the twins were thinking the same thing: *"Brendan Clark knows our names?"*

"Uh, right," Brett stammered. "Um—that was a fierce game, Brendan. You had twenty solo tackles: did you know that?"

Clark smiled faintly. "I guess I do now."

"That's not official or anything," Cody pointed out. "But we kept pretty good track."

Clark yawned. "Well, the official total will probably be less. Our stat guy usually gives at least a couple of my tackles to ATV. I think ATV threatens him."

Bart chuckled, too loudly.

"It doesn't matter though," Clark said.

"Yeah," Brett interjected. "What really matters is that you won. You spanked 'em!"

"Winning is an objective," Clark said. "I mean, they do keep score." He paused for a moment. "The party still going on in the locker room?"

"Oh, yeah," Cody said. "It's still rockin'!"

Clark stretched his hands above his head. "Well, I guess I better go join the fun." The way he said it, Cody thought, he might as well have said, "Well, I guess I better go get my wisdom teeth pulled."

Clark cleared his throat. "I had to take care of first things first though."

Brett and Bart looked at each other. "First things first?" the former asked.

"Yeah, you know, priorities. Right, Cody?"

Cody was marveling that Brendan Clark had now uttered his name twice when Brett elbowed him in the kidney. "Martin!" he whispered loudly. "The man's talkin' to you!"

"Yeah, sure," Cody said quickly. "Priorities."

"I'm not sure what either of you is talking about," Brett said. "I mean, what could be more important than celebrating with your teammates?"

"Giving thanks to God," Clark said flatly.

"Oh," Brett said, exchanging a glance with his brother.

Okay, Cody thought as he moved his eyes from the twins to Brendan Clark, *this must be what they mean by "awkward silence."*

Finally, Brett offered, "Well, I think we better get back down to the field and find our dad. You comin' Cody? You need a ride?"

"Nah. I think I'll ride home with the Porters. You guys go ahead."

The Evanses congratulated Clark again, then left the wrestling room as if they were late for dinner.

"I hope I didn't embarrass you or anything, Cody," Clark said when the twins were gone.

Cody wasn't sure what Clark meant. He answered anyway. "No. You didn't embarrass me at all. It's all good, you know."

Clark nodded slowly. "Some people can find it a little awkward to talk about their faith. That used to be me. But not anymore. God has done so much for us; it would just be a crime to not give him his props, right?"

"Right—but—" Cody felt the question forming in his mind. It was a question he had wondered about for the past few football seasons, and he really wanted it answered. *But*, he warned himself, *this is a question that could also get you concussed by the best middle linebacker in the state.*

"But?" Clark's voice was soft, patient. Nothing like the voice that commanded the Eagles in pregame warm-ups or practices. Cody allowed his gaze to fall on the figure in front of him. Especially in this light, Clark, with his boyish, rounded face, looked more like an extra from a Nickelodeon kids' show than the guy Pork Chop called "The Baddest Man in Shoulder Pads." If you saw just his head shot in a yearbook, Cody surmised, you'd think he was harmless—until you saw that head was attached to a professional wrestler's body.

Cody swallowed. He could feel Clark's eyes on him. "It's just that I've been watching you for a long time now. And when you make a big play—sack the QB or pick off a pass—you don't point at the sky. And when you score a TD, you don't kneel in the end zone like some of the guys in college and the pros do. I mean, you say you have to give God his props, but—"

Cody paused. Clark was staring at him, studying him. *This is great, Cody Martin*, he scolded himself. *It's months until wrestling season. That means once Clark kills you, they won't even find the body for a*

*long, long time. Oh, well, if I gotta get killed, I guess
I'd rather it be by Brendan Clark than Gabe Weitz.
At least Clark's a legend, not a loser.*

Clark was chuckling softly. "You know, I think I
will believe you that I had twenty tackles tonight,
no matter what the stat boy says. You're an observant guy. You know, no one else has noticed what
you have. In fact, I've heard people say I actually do
the kind of stuff you're talking about. They just
assume I do all that demonstrative stuff because I'm
a Christian."

Cody wanted to do something demonstrative at
the moment—drop to his knees and thank God for
sparing his life. But he wanted an answer to his question first, although he wasn't sure he had, in fact,
asked a question.

He looked up from the wrestling mat when he heard
Clark clear his throat. "So, Cody," the linebacker said,
"here's the deal—if I may?"

Cody shrugged, embarrassed. "Sure. I mean, I'm
interested—"

Clark smiled. "Do you think God cares who wins
football games?"

"No."

"Do you think he cares about tackle stats, touchdowns, who makes the all-state team?"

Cody wagged his head.

"Neither do I. See, all I think God cares about is who honors him. That's all I try to do in football, in the classroom, in life. When I get an A on a test, I don't point to the sky or kneel in prayer in the chemistry lab. So why would I do that kind of thing on the field? Never have. Never will. You feelin' what I'm sayin'?"

Cody shifted his feet. "I think so, but those other guys—the ones who do celebrate—"

"I'm not dissing them. As long as they do what they do to honor God, not bring attention to themselves, I'm cool with it."

Cody felt his head nodding in agreement. Clark reached out and rested a hand on his shoulder. "Well, it's been good kickin' it with you, Cody. I gotta hit the showers. You keep the faith, okay?"

"Okay," Cody said, but he didn't know if Clark heard him. Clark was already sprinting across the wrestling room toward the lockers.

-||||||-

The following Monday's practice began with Coach Morgan addressing the whole team, freshmen included. "I'll make this brief," he said. "Winston Lydell and Avery Lynn are no longer part of this football team. They violated a team rule over the weekend. You all signed a document committing to following the rules. I expect you to honor your word. There are consequences for those who don't."

The news cast a shadow over practice. Between drills, it was the only topic of conversation. Lydell and Lynn, a free safety, represented half of the Eagles' starting defensive backfield.

"Dude," Bart said to Cody as the freshmen lined up to run gassers—a series of six sprints across the width of the field—"Morgan is harsh. I mean, no warnings, no temporary suspension, just boom! One mistake and you're outta here!"

"Well," said Mark Goddard, "a rule is a rule, and a promise is a promise."

Cody smiled at Goddard, a multisport athlete like him. Goddard was still carrying about ten extra pounds around the middle, which puzzled Cody, because no one worked harder in practice. Well, no one except Pork Chop.

The freshmen were supposed to have their season opener on Thursday, but the bus carrying the Maranatha Christian School team broke down halfway between Colorado Springs and Grant. The game was rescheduled for the following Tuesday. To help alleviate his team's disappointment, Coach Vance hastily put together a scrimmage against the JV.

Cody intercepted a pass and knocked down two more, but the excitement he felt about the feats was fleeting. He hungered for real game action.

On Friday night, he rode with Mr. Porter to watch the Grant varsity face Burlington in a nonconference game. He had hoped his dad would join them, but Dad and his girlfriend, Beth, decided to see a movie instead.

Coaches Morgan and Alvin did their best to compensate for the loss of two defensive-backfield starters. They moved Paul Goddard, Mark's older brother, from strong safety to cornerback. Then, after much discussion, they named Marcus Berringer their new roving free safety. This meant he would get fewer reps at running back, but Cody knew he wouldn't care. A chance to start on the varsity came around about as often as Halley's Comet.

For a while, it looked like the "musical players" experiment would work. The Eagles led 3–0 at the end of the first half. The defense allowed a total of twenty-seven yards. Clark amassed twelve tackles. On one play, he hit the Burlington fullback so hard the fullback's helmet flew off.

Unfortunately, the Burlington coaching staff made a key halftime adjustment. The Cougars abandoned the running game in the third quarter and took to the air. One of their wideouts kept beating Goddard deep, and an overzealous Berringer committed two costly pass-interference penalties.

With the Eagles trailing 17–6, Craig Ward looked to get his team back in the game. Realizing that Burlington was exploiting Goddard's lack of speed, he cheated to the opposite side of the field on a third and eight. He made a one-handed interception of an attempted down-and-in and bolted for the end zone.

The Burlington fullback, the one Clark had blown up earlier, was ready for him. As Ward crossed the twenty, the fullback hit him flush in the right shoulder with the crown of his helmet. Ward collapsed instantaneously. He struggled to his feet moments later, his arm hanging limp at his side. He looked to the sideline and shook his head.

"Uh-oh," Mr. Porter said to Cody, "that is not good. I bet he's gone and separated that shoulder."

Mr. Porter proved to be a prophet. Ward had season-ending shoulder surgery the Monday after the game. The Eagles' defensive backfield was a shambles.

Chapter 3
The Intruder

As the Eagle freshmen went through pregame warm-ups before their rescheduled season opener, Cody noticed Coach Morgan approach Coach Alvin and Coach Vance. All their faces were somber, and they talked with their heads almost touching, as if they were telling government secrets. This was no casual "good luck, Coach!" kind of conversation.

Then, Cody felt his heart accelerate when he saw Coach Alvin point at him. At least, he feared he was the target. He looked around. No one was doing jumping jacks close to him. *Okay*, Cody tried to assure himself. *This doesn't mean anything. There could be any number of reasons Coach A is pointing at you. Maybe he's showing Coach Morgan the skinniest guy* on the team. Or pointing out the guy with the dead mom. Or maybe he's not pointing at you at all. Maybe he's pointing at Goddard, only his aim's not very good. He's not looking to call you up to varsity, so quit worrying. There's no way they're gonna start a punk freshman DB. That would be insane.

"Martin!" Cody startled at the sound of Coach Alvin's sandpaper voice. "Get over here! Chop-chop!"

Cody sprinted to the coaches, helmet in his hand. "Yes, Coach?" he said.

Alvin poked a thumb in Coach Morgan's direction. "You know this guy, right? The head honcho?"

Cody formed his words carefully. "Yes, of course, sir. Is there something I can do for you, Coach Morgan?"

A smile played at the corners of Coach Morgan's mouth. "Yes, there is, son. Play a whale of a game out there. I'll be watching."

"Yes sir," Cody said, nodding so hard that he was almost bowing. As he trotted back to his teammates, he swallowed hard. It felt like a hard-boiled egg had lodged in his throat. *Oh, boy*, he thought. *This is not good. This is* sooooo *not good. I don't need that kinda scrutiny!*

Cody lay on his back on a bench in the locker room, his chest heaving. He could feel his heart thundering not just in his chest but in his neck, in his head. On the last play of the first half, Maranatha's QB had attempted a desperation pass to the end zone, to the wideout Cody was covering. The pass was five yards short of the end zone, and Cody broke back to the ball, using his body to shield the receiver.

He locked the ball in his hands and took off like a sprinter down the right sideline. Seeing two defenders looming ahead near midfield, he angled back to the center of the field. He hurdled one of his own players—he thought it was Brett Evans—at the Maranatha forty-five and deftly sidestepped a would-be tackler at the thirty. He thought he was home free, but as he crossed the twenty, he was jerked back suddenly. Someone had clamped onto the back of his shoulder pads.

He tried to twist away, hoping to fling the defender off of him, but then someone hit him below the knees. As he fell, he hoped he wouldn't land on the ball.

He didn't. What he did do was wriggle from underneath the two Crusader defenders and sprint to the nearest referee, furiously signaling for a time-out. He had checked the clock before the play. Twenty-eight seconds had remained. Even with his adventurous romp across the field, he knew there was still time for a field goal attempt.

And Mark Goddard's kick was true, from twenty-nine yards out. He was no ATV, but he split the uprights to give the frosh Eagles a 10–7 halftime lead.

Goddard was standing by him now, blond hair plastered to his scalp. "That was some sweet pick and run-back, Cody. Thanks for giving me another field goal try. I feel bad I shanked that one in the first quarter."

Cody sat up slowly. "You put us ahead, Mark. Just keep your head down on your kicks and you'll be fine. As for the pick, the way that QB lofted it up there, I knew it was gonna be a can of corn for somebody. I was just lucky enough he put it near me."

Coach Vance called for the players to gather near a whiteboard on a mobile easel that he had parked near the showers. He didn't look like a man whose team was winning. "Some of you," he began ominously, "need to decide if you want to play high school football. Because your effort stinks. For example, Cody Martin makes a great pick and gets his skinny booty up the field in a big hurry. But does anybody make the transition from defense to offense and lay some blocks for him? Except for Mark Goddard and Brett Evans, the answer is no! Evans falls down because he wants to blow his guy up, not just impede him till Cody can get by. I can't fault that kind of effort. The point is, we should be up by a touchdown right now, not just a field goal."

Cody dared a quick scan of the locker room. Heads were hanging.

Coach Vance sipped from a water bottle, then continued. "One more thing. Paul Getman." The coach trained his eyes on the tight end/strong safety. "When the opposing QB throws the ball in the end zone, you don't tip it up in the air, going for the interception. Unless you are sure you can make the pick, you do what Martin did on the fourth play of the game—you knock the stinkin' ball down! Got that?"

Getman nodded, his eyes still trained on the floor.

The Coach diagrammed a few defensive adjustments, then sent the team back on the field. Pork Chop was waiting near the locker room entrance, smiling approvingly. "Cody Martin, you are blowin' stuff up. An interception, three pass deflections, and a sack on a corner blitz. You're a beast, my brother! Next time you come out to the farm for dinner, I'm gonna tell the Old Boy not to even cook your steak. You can just eat it raw!"

"Thanks, Chop," Cody said.

"You did only one thing wrong," Chop called from behind him as he jogged down to the field. "You shoulda scored on that I-N-T return. You gotta get your speed on next time!"

Cody chuckled. Chop was probably right. He shouldn't have been caught from behind, even if those guys hadn't run almost the whole length of the field, as he had. But the worst part of being caught wasn't that it exposed his lack of speed. When he had first felt that hand clamp on him, he thought it belonged to Gabe Weitz. *Yet another sign*, he told himself, *that you are, one by one, losing your marbles.*

The Crusaders kept the ball on the ground for most of the third quarter. They did try one shallow crossing route to the tight end, but Cody and Brett dragged him down for just a short gain.

The scoreboard remained frozen at 10–7 as the game wound down to its final fifty-eight seconds. Maranatha began a final drive at its own thirty-eight, after Goddard shanked a punt.

Two running plays moved the ball to the Grant forty, but they also used up the Crusaders' final time-outs.

"They'll have to put the ball in the air now," Brett told his teammates in the defensive huddle. "Be ready."

"One more thing," Cody said. He felt ten face masks turn in his direction. He wondered if he had ever said anything in a huddle before. He couldn't remember.

"What's up, Code?" Brett asked, prompting him.

Cody cleared his throat, hoping that some sound would emanate from his voice box. "Their QB is tired," he said. "He's floating his passes. Look for 'em to run shallow patterns and try for a catch-and-run. Or catch-and-lateral."

He saw his teammates nodding in agreement.

Maranatha lined up with no one in the backfield except for the quarterback. Two receivers flanked either side of the line. Cody took the inside receiver on the strong side. The receiver fired off the ball and ran a seven-yard down-and-in. Cody shadowed him, giving him more cushion than he normally would. He knew the team could live with a seven-yard gain to the middle of the field. In fact, such a play might run out the clock.

The Maranatha QB cocked the ball behind his ear and let it fly. Cody knew the ball wasn't intended for his man the moment it cleared the line of scrimmage. He hoped Getman, playing safety behind him, had *his* guy covered.

Suddenly, Cody found himself leaping in the air. He didn't think about it; he just jumped. There was no way he could have known that Getman's man had slipped behind him.

He felt the pebble-grain leather graze his fingertips. At first, he thought the ball would dance out of his grip, but he was able to tip it once, then secure it. His right foot touched the ground first, then his left. He paused for an instant, looking for a running lane. He had a few yards of open green in front of him to his right. He bolted in that direction.

As he ran, an image of Craig Ward flashed in his mind, and he dropped immediately to the ground. He covered the ball with his body, waiting to hear a referee's whistle.

After the two teams lined up and shook hands at midfield, the Eagles surrounded Cody and escorted him to the locker room, congratulating him and hammering him across the shoulder pads all the way.

Coach Morgan was waiting for him at the locker room entrance. "Mister Martin," he said. "Come with me."

Cody followed the coach down the hallway between the men's and women's locker rooms, his cleats clacking across the tiled floor.

At the hallway's halfway point, Coach Morgan turned to him. "That defensive holding penalty you committed in the first quarter? That was not an intelligent play. And you tried to arm tackle the fullback in the third quarter. He ran right through you. You must work on those things, understand?"

Cody nodded.

"But," Coach Morgan said, resting his hands on Cody's shoulder pads, "I believe those were the only two mistakes you made the entire game. You kept

their receivers smothered. You made two big intercep-
tions. One easy, one difficult. I'm equally impressed
with both. Too often, players muff an opportunity
when it appears easy."

Cody fought the suspicion that he was on one of
those hidden-camera shows. This one would be called
"Yeah, *right*!" It would build up people's egos, then
smash them and trample them to the ground.

Coach Morgan was speaking again, and Cody
silently chastised himself for missing his words while
he was off in fantasy land. "...that was the most
pleasing aspect of your game. Craig Ward did that last
year, you know. Made a game-saving interception,
then got himself on the ground. There's no sense in
running around getting cute and trying to run out the
clock when you're protecting a lead. I've seen too
many weird things happen. Fumbles, muffed laterals,
last-second penalties."

"I saw that Craig Ward play," Cody said, nodding
excitedly. "It was last year's homecoming. That's why
I did what I did. I remembered him. And I remember
Doug Porter saying to me after the game, 'That Ward
is one smart football player!'"

Coach Morgan glanced at his watch. Without looking up, he said, "That's what Doug Porter would be
saying now, if he'd seen you play today."

Morgan slipped past Cody and strode down the hallway. He slowed for a moment and looked over his shoulder. "Come see me tomorrow before practice. I have something I need you to do."

Cody had no shortage of offers for rides home, but he decided to walk. It was only a fifteen-minute trek, and the late-afternoon air felt good on his hair, still damp from the shower. He wondered what his dad's excuse would be this time for missing an important game. Probably, "Tuesday? Who plays football on Tuesday? I'm used to Friday and Saturday games. Sorry, buddy, I guess this one just took me by surprise."

Cody shook his head. He had thought things were changing. His father had become more involved toward the end of baseball season, but now it seemed old patterns were reestablishing themselves. His father hadn't been to a single practice, information meeting, or scrimmage. And now he had missed the season opener.

He decided to think about something more uplifting—like his conversation with Coach Morgan. What was the "something" the coach needed him to do? *It has to be something important, right? Cody tossed the possibilities around in his head. Maybe he wants me to at least practice with the varsity—give the receivers someone new to work against. I guess that would be okay. Of course, maybe all he wants is for someone to hold the Dial-a-Down markers during home games. Whatever it is, it'll be cool. Because Coach Morgan is cool.*

Martin Morgan looked about the same age as Cody's dad, forty-two. Built more like a marathon runner than a football player, Morgan had led the Grant High football team ever since Cody could remember. Unlike most of his opposing coaches, he was quiet. He didn't stalk the sidelines barking at his players, the officials, or the opposing team.

And he didn't wear a headset to communicate with other coaches. "He doesn't need guys feeding him information from the press box; he just has a feel for the game," Doug Porter had once explained to Cody and Pork Chop. "He understands football. He makes in-game adjustments like nobody's business. And he talks straight too. He doesn't blow smoke and he doesn't take cheap shots at his players, either."

I would love to play for Coach Morgan, Cody thought as he walked up his driveway. *But just not now. Maybe in one or two years—and about twenty pounds from now!*

The TV was on when he entered the front door. He was surprised to see his father in his easy chair, curtained behind his *Wall Street Journal*. The scene was typical, just not at 4:30 in the afternoon. Luke Martin was a workaholic who rarely arrived home before 7:00 p.m. And where was his dad's hopelessly old Geo? Had he actually put it in the garage?

"Hey, Dad," Cody said casually. "You're home early."

In return, Cody received only a Neanderthal grunt.

Okay, then, he thought. *Dad's not in a talkative mood. Maybe something went bad at the office today.* He paused a moment, waiting to see if his father would lower the paper and offer a more hospitable greeting. But the paper barely rustled.

"Well," Cody began again, slowly, "I'm gonna go upstairs and call Robyn. I'll be down in a few minutes, and maybe can we go to Louie's and have pizza for dinner? The game was awesome. I want to tell you about it."

Another noncommittal grunt.

Cody was halfway up the stairs when it hit him. Something was wrong. He turned around and studied his dad again. He noticed the shoes—off-brand sneakers. They had been white once but now looked as if they had been dipped in soot. They didn't look familiar, although Luke Martin rarely wore anything resembling athletic shoes. *Maybe he found those tired old kicks in the back of his closet, and he's finally going to do some yardwork*, Cody thought.

But then he noticed the jeans. They were faded so badly that they looked almost white, rather than blue. And the legs filling them were thick, testing the seams, not the spindly limbs that Cody had inherited from his dad.

Cody swallowed hard. Was the figure in the chair a friend of his dad's, maybe just waiting for him to come home? No, that didn't make sense. A friend would have introduced himself.

He thought about bounding up the remaining stairs, grabbing the phone and calling 911. But how long would it take the police to respond? And what if the phone lines had already been cut?

He eased down the stairs. "On second thought," he said, trying to keep his voice calm and measured, "I think I might shoot a few hoops before I call Robyn. Can't lose my shooting touch, you know."

He moved toward the door. The figure lowered the paper and smiled at him.

"Hello, Cody," Gabe Weitz said, with a teeth-baring smile. "I'm glad you're home."

Weitz exploded out the door and ran toward Cody. Up the road, Cody saw a minivan approaching. He froze for a moment, then scooped Maxwell into his arms. He doubted he could outrun Weitz while toting a kid, but he wasn't going to leave Little Max, as he called him, wandering in the road.

He sprinted toward the minivan, Max jostling against his chest. "Faster, Cody. Faster!" Max cried gleefully.

Tomorrow, I might laugh about this, Cody thought. *If I live to see tomorrow.*

He saw the van hit its brakes and go into a serpentine skid. He saw the panic in the driver's face. *He's trying like mad to stop, and I'm running right for him, hauling a little kid in my arms*, Cody thought. *The poor guy must think I'm on crack!*

The van stopped. The driver was out of it, striding purposefully to erase the five yards between him and Cody. "Y-young man," he stammered, "what in the world is going on here?"

"Cody givin' me a ride!" Max offered helpfully. "Fun!"

The driver looked at Max and smiled. The smile vanished the instant he focused on Cody again. "Are you this boy's brother? What are you thinking—running like a madman down the middle of the street? Is this man coming up to us the boy's father?"

Cody felt the human equivalent of a system overload. He wasn't sure which question to tackle first. "Found ... Max in ... street," he managed. "Had to get him outta there."

The driver spat on the street. "Running down the middle of the road is not the way to get someone out of danger."

"You there," he was addressing Weitz now. "Can you shed some light on this? Or do I need to get my cell out of the van and call the police?"

"Police!" Cody shouted, as if it were the secret word of the day on a radio contest. "Yes, call the police! Please. This guy," he pointed an accusing forefinger at Weitz, "he broke into my house. He attacked me."

The driver took two steps back toward the van. Cody felt worry encircling him like a python. The guy wasn't very big; maybe he was scared now. Maybe he was going to scurry inside his minivan and speed away.

Cody heaved a relieved sigh when the driver poked his hand inside the van and snatched his cell phone. He hit one key and held the phone to his ear. *I wonder if he has the police on speed dial*, Cody thought.

While the driver waited for his call to connect, he stared at Weitz, who was bent over at the waist, hands on his knees, panting and coughing. "Is what this boy says true, sir?" the man asked.

Weitz looked up, held his palms up, and shrugged. "I don't know what he's talking about. I saw this guy running down the road with a kid in his arms. The kid looked scared. So I decided to run after him to check it out."

"You're a liar!" Cody spat the words out like rotten food. The anger in his voice shocked him.

Cody turned back to the driver, who was mumbling something into his cell phone. "Okay, then, see you in a few." He smiled at Cody and Weitz, but there was no humor in the smile. "Just called a friend of mine. Paul Vance. Coaches football at the high school. He'll be here in less than five minutes. So you both sit tight. Now I'm calling the police."

Cody looked at Weitz. "Mr. Vance is my football coach. We'll see who he believes. You are so busted. I can't believe you broke into our house!" Cody pictured his sturdy coach, with a pushed-in boxer's nose. He looked like he had been in a few scraps. Meanwhile, he saw something in Weitz's eyes—panic.

Slowly, Weitz began backing away. Then he turned and jogged back down the street. "Hey, wait just a minute!" the driver called. But then apparently a voice on his cell phone interrupted him.

Cody lowered Max to the ground as he watched Weitz climb into a battered Nissan truck that was parked in the street opposite Cody's house. *I wondered whose Loser-Mobile that was,* Cody thought.

-||||||-

Coach Vance arrived five minutes after Weitz drove away. Cody explained the entire saga. The harassment, the threats, the beat-down from Doug Porter. The coach's face grew progressively redder as Cody went on.

When Cody finished, Coach Vance looked him in the eyes. "Martin, you need to tell your father about this tonight. You need to report this to the police right away. This Weitz fella has broken the law. That needs to be dealt with."

"There you are, ya little snot!" The abrasive voice of Max's mother preempted Cody's response. "When are you going to learn to quit creeping out of the house?"

Max looked at his mom and smiled. "Cody give me a ride!" he said. "Cody strong!"

"Yeah, whatever," Mrs. Enger said, slinging Max on her hip. "Thanks, Toby, for tracking down this little twerp. Again."

"It's Cody," he said softly, but he doubted that she heard him.

"That's what I like to see," Coach Vance said when the departing duo was out of earshot, "a mom with a cigarette in one hand and a little kid in the other." He put one hand on his jawbone, the other on the opposite temple, and gave his neck a sharp twist. The resulting crack made Cody shudder. "Anyhow, remember what I said about the police."

"But Coach," Cody protested. "Didn't your friend already call them?"

The coach shook his head. "That was just a bluff, right, Irv?"

"Yeah," the driver said sheepishly. "I just called for the time and temperature. I figured Paul was better than the police. He's not worried about the whole brutality thing."

"That's right," Coach Vance said. "Videotape me putting the beat-down on some loser, and I'll put it on the Net and charge $29.95 per viewing!"

Cody paced the living room waiting for his dad to get home. It was 8:30 before he pulled in the driveway. He tugged Beth behind him, holding her hand like a teacher leading a little kid on a field trip.

"I think I'm gonna puke," Cody muttered.

He stood in the front-door entrance. "Dad," he said as soon as the door opened, "I have to tell you something!"

"Whoa there, buddy-o," his dad chuckled. "Let us get inside first. Besides, we have something to tell *you*. And there's no way your news can trump ours."

"But, Dad—"

"Cody," his dad's voice was uncharacteristically stern. "Don't be rude. Please sit down."

Cody shrugged helplessly and obeyed.

"Cody," his father began, "you know that Beth and I have been together for quite some time now. And you know we've grown quite close to each other. And Beth has grown quite fond of you as well." As if on cue, Cody's dad looked to Beth, who smiled at Cody and nodded.

His dad was talking again. It sounded as if he were reading a prepared speech. "I have told you the simple truth that I am not the kind of person who was meant to be alone. And I believe that God acknowledged that and brought Beth into my life. And so, after much thought and prayer, I have asked Beth to marry me. Thank goodness, tonight she said yes. We shall be married soon. Most likely early November."

Cody tried to let the words sink in. That was just two-and-a-half months away. *Why so soon!* were the words that formed in his mind, but he decided they were best kept there.

"Cody," his dad said, forcing his mouth into a smile, "don't you have anything to say?"

"Sorry, Dad. I guess I'm just surprised. Plus, it's been kind of a weird day. Congratulations, really, to both of you." He moved to his dad and hugged him. Beth was next. *Still wearing too much perfume*, Cody thought as he embraced her awkwardly. She raised on her tiptoes and kissed the top of his head.

Man, I hate when she does that, he thought.

"Would you like to see the *ring*?" she asked, her voice going up about an octave on the word "ring."

"Sure," Cody said. *So much for "Thou shalt not lie,"* he thought.

After Beth dangled her left hand in front of Cody's face, she and his dad began gushing about their wedding plans. Finally, his dad drew in a deep breath and leveled his eyes at Cody. "And buddy-o," he said, his voice cracking around the edges, "I want you to be my best man. That would mean so much to me."

"Sure, Dad," Cody answered, wondering if his smile looked as fake and forced as it felt.

His father thanked him, then launched into a detailed description of the best man's responsibilities.

When that discourse was finally over, his father stood. "I'm going to take Beth home now. Maybe stop somewhere for coffee and dessert. Oh—what was your news, Cody? I hope it's as good as ours."

Cody watched the two of them, arms around each other, smiling like they were doing a toothpaste commercial. "Oh, it's nothing, Dad. Just had a really good game this afternoon. That's all."

"Way to go, tiger," his dad said. It sounded like a line from a high school play.

"Yeah, way to go," Beth added. Then they were gone, giggling all the way to the car.

Cody stood sandwiched between Paul Goddard and a lanky junior named Dilts on the south goal line of the practice field. Brett, next to Dilts, shifted his weight nervously from one foot to the other.

Coach Morgan and Coach Alvin faced them. The rest of the team stood along the east sideline looking on. "As you know," the head coach began, "we have been decimated by injuries. Because of this, I have adjusted our defense from a forty-three set to a fifty-three. As often as we can, we'll go with three DBs and put an extra guy up front. But three of the teams remaining on our schedule have fine quarterbacks and good receivers. We can't give them a skeleton defensive backfield to pick apart. In those cases, we'll need two corners and two safeties."

Cody exchanged a quick glance with Brett. They both knew what was coming.

"Our challenge," Coach Alvin added, after getting an approving nod from Coach Morgan, "is that we are seriously hurting at cornerback. Dalton Rhodes has plenty of corner experience, and we'll be okay with him replacing Craig Ward. Goddard, you have done an adequate job of moving from safety to corner. But we are concerned about your speed. So we're going to stage a little race. We know what your forty-yard-dash times are wearing shorts. But we need to see who is the fastest in full pads."

With that, both coaches stepped aside. "It's one hundred yards to the other goal line, gentlemen," Coach Alvin said. "On my whistle, I want you all to run like crazy. Whoever wins doesn't have to run gassers tonight. And he gets to play some games as starting varsity cornerback."

Dilts poked his hand up. "So does that mean, like, we're gonna race?"

Coach Alvin stared at Dilts. "No, genius, it means we're gonna bake cookies!" He looked to his boss. "Coach Morgan, was I unclear about anything I said?"

The head coach's face was expressionless. "No," he said, "I don't believe you were."

"I didn't think so. Now, if there are no more questions, may we begin?"

"Yes sir," Dilts mumbled.

"Are you sure Mister Dilts? Are you clear on which direction you are running? On how far?"

Dilts nodded.

Coach Alvin blew a shrill, rippling blast on his whistle. Cody knew he was first off the line. He had watched the coach inhale and did his best to get a fast start. He knew he would need it.

Dilts pulled alongside him as they crossed the forty-yard line. He had a long stride, but from the desperate, rattling breaths he was taking, Cody knew he was tiring. Sure enough, as they hit midfield, Dilts's form started to break down. He was cooked.

As they neared the other forty, Cody felt Goddard on his heels. Then, five yards later, Goddard was even with him. Goddard looked over and said "See you at the club, Code," then accelerated by him.

Before the comment, Cody was ready to concede the race to the senior. He didn't want to play varsity football as a freshman, and—although he disliked losing a race—it was no disgrace to be outrun by a senior.

But "See you at the club"? That was cocky. That was disrespect. Cody pumped his arms furiously. He lengthened his stride but still fought to keep his legs turning over at maximum rate. Eighteen yards from the finish, Goddard began to tie up. Cody drew even with him at the twelve. Goddard tried to find another gear, but he had used them all. In desperation, the senior lunged for the goal line.

Cody didn't lunge. He kept his legs moving. He beat Goddard by half a yard and had to clutch the goal post to keep from crumpling to the turf. Gulping for air, he looked back down the field. He wondered what had happened to Brett, until he saw him limping to the sideline, holding his right hamstring.

Cody expected Pork Chop to be the first one there to congratulate him, but Chop couldn't run a 4.5 forty like Brendan Clark. For a moment, Cody feared that Clark was going to tackle him, but he stopped just short of contact. "That's the way to get your speed on, Martin!" Clark barked. "You sure you're just a freshman?"

"Yeah," Cody said sincerely.

Pork Chop was next in line. For a moment, he appeared to be searching for words. Finally, he belched softly and said, "Welcome to the varsity, bro."

Coach Alvin let a few more well-wishers congratulate Cody before he cut in. He handed Cody a cup of water. "Drink this," he commanded. "Then follow me. We have a lot of work to do."

Coach Alvin spent most of the practice with his defensive backs. He explained that when facing run-oriented teams, Paul Goddard would play one corner with Rhodes at the other. Berringer would represent the team's last line of defense as a roving safety. When battling a team that favored the pass, Goddard would move back to strong safety, his natural position, and Cody would start alongside Rhodes.

"I'm not gonna blow any smoke up your skirts," Coach Alvin said, pointing a finger at Cody, then Rhodes. "Both of you are two or three steps slower than Winston Lydell. And you're a whole bunch of steps slower than Craig Ward. His 4.4 in the forty is a team record. So you're going to have to give receivers more cushion that we'd like. And you, Mr. Martin, are going to have to learn how to get low and knock guys' legs out from under them. You're not gonna be wanting to hit anybody high. I got a cat almost as big as you."

Chapter 5

Road Kill

Lightweight. Sissy-boy. Powder puff. Moron. Hapless idiot. Lying on his bed on Friday night, Cody ran through the list of names Coach Alvin had called him during his first three varsity practices. He chuckled to himself. A year ago, in middle school, Coach Smith had used similar terminology, and it had hurt. But there was something about the way Coach Alvin tossed the terms around, almost like nicknames. There was no venom dripping off them.

And Coach Alvin peppered everyone with monikers. When ATV would fumble during a scrimmage, he became "SUV" or "Minivan." One missed tackle and Jeff Tucker became "Jeff Tuckered Out."

Brendan Clark was the only player who had escaped the whiplash that was Coach Alvin's tongue. And that was because Cody hadn't seen Clark make a mistake or fail to hustle during even one drill.

With Ward injured, Clark always won the end-of-practice gassers, the grueling sprints across the width of the football field—six or seven times in a row. It wasn't an unfamiliar sight to see him clinging to the chain link fence after practice heaving his lunch.

Just before Cody slipped into sleep, he prayed, "Thank you, God, that I made varsity. This is the coolest thing to happen in a long time. Not to seem ungrateful or anything, but Lost Valley is a grind-it-out running team, and I wouldn't mind it at all if they stick to the run all afternoon tomorrow. Amen, and go Eagles!"

Lost Valley tried to surprise the Eagles by trying to hit a receiver on a drag pattern over the middle on the first play of the game. That was the first of their two pass attempts for the entire game.

The Vikings featured a hulking 230-pound fullback named Nash who touched the ball almost every play. By double-teaming Brendan Clark, also on almost every play, Lost Valley was able to spring Nash for several big gains.

ATV did his best to keep Grant in the game, piling up 188 yards on twenty-six bruising carries. But the team missed the luxury of putting Craig Ward in at receiver when they needed a big gain. Ward also returned kickoffs and punts. His backup, unfortunately, was Winston Lydell.

Grant trailed 14–7 and had the ball late in the fourth quarter, but ATV was too gassed to run effectively, and Dean Hammond, the Eagle QB, misfired on three straight passes to end the game.

"That's just great," ATV snapped in the locker room after the game. "We get beat by Lost Valley. That doesn't even sound like a school. Sounds like a salad dressing!"

It was only five o'clock when the yellow school bus pulled into the Grant High School parking lot. Cody, who hadn't played at all, decided he would go for a run when he got home. *Might as well get some exercise today*, he reasoned.

Man, it feels good to be running without all my foot-ball gear on, Cody thought. *And it feels good to not be worrying about hitting somebody—or being hit.*

He was running east, about two miles out of town, he guessed. *Two more miles*, he told himself, *and I'll* head back. He ran facing traffic along Highway 7, although there really *wasn't* any traffic. He had seen only one car zoom by him since he left the Grant city limits behind.

Just as Cody took a swig from his water bottle, he stumbled on the chewed-up asphalt along the road's narrow shoulder. He managed to keep his feet, but he also managed to snort water up his nose. He felt his nostrils burn and tried to suppress a sneeze.

Well, he sighed inwardly, *this* was *a perfect run. Man, this shoulder is really ragged over here. Think I'll cross to the other side.*

Drew Phelps had warned Cody about running with traffic, but Cody wasn't worried. Traffic had been less than sparse, and he figured he would have plenty of time to move off the right shoulder, or even cross back across the road, if he heard a vehicle coming.

He angled across the asphalt. It felt surprisingly soft under his feet in the late-September heat. Once on the other side of the road, he settled into a smooth pace again. The running felt almost effortless. He let his mind drift. He wondered if he would be able to run a sub-five-minute mile when track season rolled around. He thought about basketball season too. Mr. Clayton, his eighth-grade coach, had moved up to the high school, where he was coaching basketball and track as well as teaching PE. Clayton had been the first coach to truly show confidence in him. He was eager to have another shot at rewarding that confidence.

He reminded himself that he should tell Coach Clayton about Gabe Weitz's unwelcome visit. When Cody finally cornered his dad and told him about it, Luke Martin assured his son that he would "look into it." But Cody wasn't sure there had been any follow-through until this morning. His dad delivered the news—an officer would come to the Martin house to take a statement later that evening.

Cody wondered what the experience would be like—and if his dad would show up on time as promised—or whether the commitment would get lost among the wedding plans. He wondered if he would be able to tell his story clearly to a stern-faced officer in blue, who would then find Weitz and lock him up. "Can't wait to see that loser in handcuffs," Cody muttered.

Most of all Cody thought about football. *I wonder if I'll see some varsity action next week. I have to admit I'm a little disappointed that I didn't get in the game today. I thought I'd be relieved, but—*

Cody sensed trouble when he heard the vehicle behind him gun its engine. He whipped his head around just as the battle-scarred old Nissan pickup veered onto the shoulder, spitting gravel and devouring the distance between them.

He recognized the truck immediately. It had been parked across the street the day Weitz invaded the Martin home. Cody half whispered his favorite prayer— "Help!"—and looked for an escape route. Beyond the shoulder of the road lurked a sharp drop-off into high wild grass. The grass partially camouflaged a makeshift barbed wire fence that guarded a field of some sort that had roundish green plants about knee high—and fat as medicine balls.

The truck was only about fifty yards from him now, closing fast. Cody leaped from the road, wondering where—and how—he would land. *On my feet, someplace soft would be nice*, he thought as he flew through the air. The roar of the truck engine filled his ears, his chest.

He felt the outside of his right foot touch down— and slide on the slick grass. He tucked and rolled, half expecting to either be flattened by Weitz's truck or shredded by the barbed wire. He risked a glance back toward the road.

The truck whizzed by him fish-tailing wildly. Cody heard a succession of click-click-clicks as Weitz snapped a series of reflector poles as if they were matchsticks.

Then Weitz must have lost control. The truck lunged off the shoulder and tumbled and rolled, three, maybe four times. Cody lost count.

Cody was on his feet now, so close to the barbed wire fence that he could use the top strand to steady himself. He watched the truck come to rest on its wheels. "This is real," he heard himself whisper, as he slowly stepped his way back up to the shoulder. "This is really real."

He trotted slowly, warily, toward the truck. *If Weitz pops out of that truck and comes after me,* he thought, *I'm going the other way—fast. And I think I have enough adrenaline rushing through me to run a four-minute mile right now!*

As he picked up his speed, he noticed a sharp twinge in his left ankle. It wasn't much more painful than a bee sting. It wouldn't slow him down. He'd run on lots worse.

He studied the truck carefully. It had rumbled through the fence, taking down a whole section before it finally stopped. There was no movement from inside and no smoke from under the hood. He wondered if it would suddenly explode in flames, like in the movies. The truck seemed lifeless, but he couldn't be sure.

When he pulled even with the truck, he stopped running. Carefully, he stepped down from the shoulder and began making his way toward Weitz. He lifted his knees high; he didn't want to trip at a time like this.

He drew within ten yards of the truck and stopped. He could see that Weitz was slumped over the steering wheel—he wasn't moving. Cody listened. The engine wasn't running, and there was no hissing or gurgling.

Stepping warily again, Cody had to remind himself to breathe. His heart was doing a drum solo in his chest. In the truck he saw blood spattered everywhere. He sniffed. He smelled beer, but no gasoline.

"Weitz," he said, poking his head into the truck. His voice sounded loud and foreign. "Can you hear me?"

Weitz didn't respond. Cody wanted to pull him off the steering wheel, but he remembered something he'd heard about not moving an accident victim in case of a neck injury. He couldn't remember where he'd heard the advice—probably a TV show.

He studied Weitz's massive torso for a minute, looking for signs of breathing. But with the big man hunched over, Cody could discern nothing. Tentatively, he moved his left hand toward Weitz's chest.

If he wakes up and grabs me or something, Cody thought, *I'm gonna need some new running shorts.*

He slid his hand between the steering wheel and Weitz's chest, placing it where he thought his attacker's heart would be. He paused. He felt a faint, rhythmic beat.

He's alive, Cody thought. *The guy who just tried to kill me is alive.*

He turned and studied the road to the north and south. He thought he might have heard a car whip by moments ago, but he wasn't sure. *If there was a car*, he wondered, *they must have seen the accident, right?*

He turned his attention to Weitz again. Still no movement. Cody raised his eyes to the sky. He felt a tug-of-war in his head over what to do next. Stay with Weitz and try to administer some type of first aid? Maybe try to drag him out of the truck, just in case it caught fire? Or sprint like mad back toward town? Nick Baker's gas station and convenience store was only about a mile back.

God, he prayed earnestly, *I just don't know what to do. I don't really know any first aid, so I'm thinkin' I should run for help. But I don't know if I can just leave Weitz here. If you could send somebody to help me—please.*

He looked back to the road. It was empty in both directions. He exhaled shakily and tried the driver's-side door to see if it would open. It resisted at first but then gave way with a metallic creak that sent a shiver shooting down his spine. He half expected Weitz to tumble out at his feet, but there was no movement.

Cody dropped to his knees, trying to get a better look at Weitz from underneath. Most of the blood appeared to be coming from his nose, which Cody figured he had smashed on the steering wheel, or maybe the windshield, which was now a spiderweb of cracks.

"Weitz," he said again, trying to fill his voice with authority, assurance. "I hope you can hear me. Look, I'm going to run for help. I'm running to Baker's to call an ambulance—maybe I'll be able to flag down a car on the way. So if you can hear me, hang on, okay? I'm gonna get help. I'm gonna pray for you. You should pray too."

Cody placed a hand on Weitz's shoulder for just a moment, then turned and bounded toward the road.

"Okay, God," Cody gasped as he struggled to find a fast pace that he could sustain for a while, "I guess I'm doing the right thing, but this is trippy. Help Weitz— hang on. After all that's happened, it would be cool if he could survive this and turn his life around."

Cody did a half turn, running backward for a few steps so he could look back at the crash site. Still no truck in flames.

I wish Pork Chop could see this, he thought. *Not so he'd think I was a hero or anything, but so he'd learn that God does make a difference in a person's life. Because if it weren't for God, I'd be really tempted to leave Weitz's sorry carcass out there.*

Cody quieted his thoughts for a moment. He thought he heard the distant hum of tires on asphalt. He strained his eyes, studying the ribbon of highway ahead of him.

Then he saw it. A gray dot, coming his way. "All right," he panted. "Help at last!"

The dot drew closer. It was a small sedan. Maybe a Civic or a Corolla.

He began waving his hands above his head—as if doing jumping jacks. The car was only a football field away now but not slowing down. Cody waved even more frantically.

The car gave two short bursts on the horn—"hello honks," his mom had called them, as it sped by. Then he heard a fading female voice, "Yeah, we see ya, little hottieeeeee!"

Cody wagged his head in frustration. "Never thought I'd be bummed to hear something like that," he gasped.

When he saw another car approaching, he knew he would have to be more assertive. He moved from the shoulder to the middle of the oncoming traffic lane. *Please, God*, he pleaded, *don't let me get flattened by a car while trying to save Weitz's life. That would be just too weird and sad. I'm trying to do the right thing, but I don't wanna become roadkill on that guy's account!*

As the vehicle drew closer, Cody realized it wasn't a car. It was a motorcycle—a big one. He went into waving mode again, whipping his arms around like a crazed aerobics instructor.

"Thank God," he panted, as he heard the driver gearing down.

The Harley-Davidson was as big as a horse. Cody marveled at its size as the driver maneuvered his hog to the shoulder.

Cody waited till the driver killed the engine before gasping, "Accident—Call 911."

The driver, clean-shaven and thinner than Cody's stereotype of Harley men, slid a pair of dark sunglasses up to his slightly receding hairline. "Accident?" he said calmly. "Where?"

Cody turned and stabbed his right forefinger to the east. "Back there."

He wanted to say more but found it hard to link more than a few words at a time. He wasn't sure if it was exhaustion or panic. "About a half mile."

The driver nodded and angled his Harley toward town. He slid forward on his seat. "Hop on," he said. It sounded like a command, not a suggestion.

◦-||||||-◦

Cody slid off the bike as soon as it rolled and crunched to a stop in Baker's gravel parking lot. Nick Baker was at the counter. Cody pushed past a mother and two pudgy, waist-high twins to get to him.

"Mr. Baker," he said, his voice hoarse. "Call police. Ambulance. There's a wreck!"

Mr. Baker kept his eyes on Cody as he reached under the counter and produced a cell phone. "How many cars?" he mouthed to Cody.

Cody looked at him helplessly. "Huh?" he said.

"In the wreck," Mr. Baker said, annoyance creeping into his voice.

"Idiot," Cody mumbled, labeling himself, not Mr. Baker. "One," he said. "Just one. It's Gabe Weitz."

Cody gripped the counter with both hands. He listened as Mr. Baker reported the accident. Occasionally, the store owner looked to Cody to confirm something or to provide missing information. Finally, he pushed a button on the cell phone and returned it to its place.

He looked at Cody and nodded. "Help is on the way," he said.

Cody turned and sank to the floor, gulping the disinfectant-laced air. He wondered how long it would be before he heard the catlike yowl of sirens. From his sitting position, he was almost eye-to-eye with the twins. They were both studying him, with a mixture of fear and curiosity. Finally, one of them tugged on his mother's running shorts. "Is that boy sick?" he asked.

Cody and Pork Chop sat in a back booth at Dairy Delight on a Sunday following a morale-sapping 10–8 Saturday afternoon defeat at Lincoln. Coupled with a narrow homecoming win over St. Stevens, Grant's record stood at 2–3. The team's goal of a league title was drifting from the realm of possibility. Chop looked tired. He sported a gash over his left eye. His helmet had been ripped from his head during an all-out blitz late in the St. Stevens game, but he continued to battle, taking on two hard-charging pass-rushers.

But Chop wasn't interested in football. His eyes were intent on Cody. He leaned forward, resting his elbows on the table. "So, dawg," he said, deep-set brown eyes widening. "Tell me what it was like."

Cody drew in a deep breath. "Well, Dad drives me to the prison. We go to this reception window, kind of like the ticket windows at the movie theaters. There's a tired-looking guy sitting there. He pushes a form to me and says 'Fill this out.'"

When I'm done, Dad and I pass through a metal detector into this huge room. People are milling around, including a woman with two little boys, who take turns socking each other in the arm—harder each time. A guard directs me to a cubicle, kind of like the ones in the library, only when I sit down I'm staring at a Plexiglas wall. On the other side of the wall is a cubicle just like mine. It's like I'm looking in a mirror, but I'm missing from my own reflection."

Pork Chop raised his eyebrows. "Trippy," he said. "Then what?"

"A door opens on the other side of the glass. A line of scary-looking dudes in orange jumpsuits files in. In order, they start filling up the cubicles. The people on my side of the room start pointing and shouting, pushing past each other to get to the right cubicle. Weitz is last in line. I sit opposite him. He looks tired. But he's put on some muscle. Been hitting the weights, I figure. I pick up this phone. There's one just like it in his cube. He says, 'Hey.' His voice sounds all tinny and faraway, even though he's three feet from me."

Pork Chop drummed his fingers on the tabletop. "And?"

"He starts to talk, but without looking at me. He mumbles, 'What do you want?' No apologies. He doesn't ask if I got hurt when he tried to run me down. I ask him if he's okay, and he looks at me for just a second. 'Well, I'm in jail. You call *that* okay?'"

Pork Chop coughed. "What a loser."

Cody closed his eyes for a moment. "Yeah, I was expecting something more from him. But that's all he's got. He hangs up his intercom phone, pushes his chair back, and walks away."

Pork Chop took a long pull from the double straws he had plunged in his chocolate shake. "That is one freaky dream, dawg. And you say you've had it twice?"

"Yeah. And it was almost exactly the same both times. The only difference is that the first time, it was my mom who drove me to the prison."

"So, Code, do you think that's the way it might have gone down—if Weitz had lived and the police had arrested him?"

Cody exhaled slowly. He imagined Weitz regaining consciousness and staggering to the highway. He wondered if it was the injuries or the alcohol—or both—that made him suddenly lurch into the path of an oncoming Peterbilt semitruck. "Maybe," he said sadly. "I was hoping he could turn his life around. Be a different kind of person. You know, I told him to pray—when I went up to his truck after the wreck. I've wondered a lot if he heard me. I hope he did."

Pork Chop narrowed his eyes. "Why?"

"So he could be forgiven."

"But, dawg, think of how he terrorized us! He tried to kill you. He doesn't deserve to be forgiven."

"That's the point, Chop. None of us deserves it."

Pork Chop finished his shake with a long, loud

slurp. "I don't know about you, dawg. The stuff you say sometimes, it keeps me awake at night."

Cody leveled his eyes at his friend. "Good," he said.

Chapter 6

Nowhere to Hide

World History had quickly become Cody's least favorite high school class. To Cody, Mr. Dellis, with his dark, slicked-down hair and round glasses, bore an eerie resemblance to Dr. Octopus, Spider-Man's arch enemy. In reality, however, the teacher had a different enemy: Christianity.

"I will teach you things the textbooks don't have the guts to report," he had told his class on the first day of school. "I am going to teach you history as it actually was, not the way certain groups try to spin it. I don't mean to offend anyone, but I am certain that will happen. That's what results when you are committed to giving the unvarnished facts and your

unbiased opinions about them. I will make some of
you uncomfortable, but that is part of the educa-
tional process."

Cody had nodded approvingly upon hearing these
words. "Sounds to me like this class will be cool," he
said to Robyn and Pork Chop after the first class. "I'd
kinda like to learn some stuff that isn't in the history
books—get the real inside scoop, you know?"

Robyn had narrowed her sky-blue eyes, as if deep
in thought. "I don't know, Cody," she said slowly.
"Something's kind of bothering me."

Cody shrugged. "What could be bothering you, Hart?
It was just a bunch of introductory stuff."

"Well for one thing," she said, "there is no such
thing as an 'unbiased opinion.' There's a reason they're
called opinions, you know."

Pork Chop smiled at Cody. "She's got a point, dawg.
You should listen to her more—that's my unbiased
opinion anyway."

"Thank you, Deke," Robyn said. "I couldn't agree
more."

Cody rolled his eyes.

As the school days piled up, Mr. Dellis gave more
and more of his "unbiased" opinions: "The Bible glori-
fies war and demeans women." "The Bible is filled with
contradictions." "The Bible is a second-rate source of

history, at best." "The Bible promotes racism." "The most horrific atrocities in world history have been carried out in the name of Christianity and other similar religions."

Midway through the first semester, Mr. Dellis folded his hands in front of him after finishing a tirade about "rightwing politicians and their heinous abuse of power" and asked, "Anyone care to respond? I am open to dissenting opinions—"

Cody saw Robyn's hand shoot up. He knew the moment was coming. *Ah, Mr. Dellis,* he thought, *you just poked your hand into the lion's cage once too often.*

"Yes, I have a question," Robyn said, pushing her Perry Ellis glasses up her nose. Her voice had that slight quake in it that meant she was about one Fahrenheit degree short of a boil over. "Is this World History class—or Intro to Religious Bigotry?"

"Ms. Hart," Mr. Dellis scolded, "I hardly think that tone is appropriate."

Robyn arched her thin eyebrows. "But you just said you were open to dissenting opinions. You are open, aren't you?"

Mr. Dellis smiled. "I see I've touched a nerve here. Perhaps I should clarify myself. Ms. Hart, I am not trying to offend you or anyone else in this class who might share your belief system." Cody was pretty sure Mr. Dellis shot him a glance as he finished his sentence. "My point," the teacher continued, "is merely to show that Christianity has not been, by and large, a positive force in world history, including American history. I am happy to entertain facts to the contrary. But only facts, not borderline insubordination. Understand, Ms. Hart?"

Cody looked at Robyn sitting in the desk next to his, near the front of the classroom. Her jaw dropped and he could hear her gasp with exasperation. The message was clear: Are you going to help me out here or not, Cody Martin?

Cody turned to the front of the class. He kept his eyes focused on the clock at the front of the room. In nine minutes the class would be over. *This is your fight, Hart*, he thought. *I'm not going to get dragged into it. I didn't take this class to debate religion with some guy three times my age. I'd just end up looking like a fool anyway. Mr. Dellis is smart. Oily and kinda creepy, but smart.*

Cody nearly fell out of his chair when Pork Chop, sitting at the desk directly behind his, finally broke the uneasy silence. "I've just been sitting here thinking about what you said, Mr. Dellis," Chop began, "and I have to disagree."

Mr. Dellis walked toward Pork Chop's desk. "Can you back up your position, Mr. Porter?"

"I never talk unless I can back up what I say," came the response. "You know when you said Christianity hasn't been a positive force in American history? Well, what about Abraham Lincoln? I probably wouldn't be sitting here right now if not for him, and he was a deeply religious dude."

Mr. Dellis smiled dismissively. "Ah, but Mr. Porter, who says that Lincoln's faith had anything to do with his humanitarianism? He was always deeply sensitive when it came to the plights of other people. He possessed an almost innate sense of equality."

"I'm sorry, sir, but that's simply not true." Pork Chop's voice rang with genuine respect. "You see, only a couple years before he was elected president, Lincoln went on the record saying that 'Negroes' shouldn't be allowed to vote, serve on juries, or hold public office. He even said they shouldn't marry white people. But, later on, obviously, he changed his heart. A lot of people believe his faith was the cause of it." He paused and looked at Cody. "Right, dawg?"

Cody felt his face growing hot. He tried to think of something to say.

Then from the back of the room, Terry Alston, Pork Chop's rival for best all-around freshman male athlete, interrupted. "How do you know all of this, Chop? You're just a dumb lineman."

"Oh, brother," Cody muttered to himself, "here we go again. But at least the heat's off me."

Pork Chop half turned in his chair to face Alston, who was sitting to the left and behind him. Chop let out a short, humorless laugh. "Excuse me, TA. *Dumb* lineman?"

"Look," Alston said quickly, "I'm not disrespecting you. You know I respect your game. You're a big strong dude. I'm just sayin' it doesn't take a genius to ram into another big guy all day."

Pork Chop appeared genuinely amused. "Oh really," he said. He appeared ready to eject from his seat and make Terry Alston's dentist very wealthy.

Mr. Dellis, perhaps sensing a potential battle royal in his classroom, jumped in. "Now, Mr. Porter, let's remember what I said about respecting dissenting opinions. I don't know a lot about football, but I think all that Mr. Alston is saying is—"

"—See, that's my problem, Mr. Dellis," Pork Chop countered. "You don't know football. Neither does TA. He's just too pretty to play it I guess. If you did, you wouldn't use the words 'dumb' and 'lineman' in the same sentence. An offensive lineman has to be one of the smartest guys on the field."

"You've gotta be kidding," Alston scoffed.

Pork Chop looked to Mr. Dellis, "May I, sir?"

Mr. Dellis nodded and smiled. Cody's mom had a name for smiles like that: cat that ate the canary.

Pork Chop stood in front of the class as smiling and confident as a gameshow host. "It would take way too long to explain all the intricacies of an offensive lineman's responsibilities," he began, "so I'm just going to give you a little glimpse into the world of the Midnight Cowboy, lineman extraordinaire. It's a pressure-filled world, because I play left tackle. That means I have to protect the quarterback's blind side every game or he ends up in a body bag.

"Let's see, I think I'll pick a play from the third quarter of our win over Mill Creek last weekend. It's a third and six, and Hammond, our QB, calls I-right flex—dog right split. On three. See, that's our basic formation. Two running backs in the I formation. One tight end, two wideouts. But when Hammond says 'right split,' that tells Butcher, the tight end, to line up about five yards from the tackle instead of right next to him like he usually does.

"The word 'right' in 'right split' means that the formation is strong to the right—because that's where the tight end is. It also tells the two wideouts which patterns to run. You keeping up with me so far?"

Pork Chop looked to Alston, who frowned and nodded.

"Okay, that's good. 'Cuz I'm just getting started. Now Hammond is going to take a five-step drop, and his first option is a shallow out pattern to Butcher. All of this is going through my head when I get to the line and face off against Jonathon Harper, a 250-pound monster who's three years older than I am. But, for me, the key word in the play Hammond called is 'dog.' That means the line will slide to the strong side, and I'll be mano-a-mano against Harper. Unless, of course, Creek decides to stunt, and their end and tackle switch spots on the snap. Or they could blitz, and a DB will come up and shoot in behind Harper. Then I take one of the guys and ATV, our fullback, blocks the other one."

Mr. Dellis sighed, pulled a tissue from his pocket, and dabbed at his forehead. He replaced the tissue, then sat on his desk. "Is that it?" he asked hopefully.

Pork Chop belched and shook his head. "Ha. Not even close. See, on this particular play, I get to the line, and I see Harper to my left, with no one lined up against Cook—he's our left guard—and my homey. It doesn't look like their strong-side linebacker is going to blitz, and they're not bringing up a safety either. So I'm thinkin' what's up here? What's their game?"

Cody studied Mr. Dellis. It looked like he might get up from the desk and try to regain control of his classroom. But Cody knew his friend wasn't done yet, so he asked, "Chop, how did you solve the mystery?"

Pork Chop winked at him. "I'm getting to that. See, by this time I have battled Harper for thirty-two plays. I've learned that he has decent speed for such a big tank, but he's a creature of habit. He hasn't given me an inside move all afternoon. So I'm just about positive that he's going to try to barrel around the outside and outrun me to Hammond. I'm in my two-point stance, so Harper knows that we're either gonna pass or run a draw play. So I'm not gonna charge right at him in run-block mode. I have my left foot behind my right one because I need a quick start. I gotta get moving backward as soon as the ball is snapped.

"I'm moving as soon as Hammond begins to pronounce the 'h' in 'hut.' I know his cadence like my own. Harper blasts out of his stance. I slide into position. My footwork is perfect. He's going outside again, just as I figured. I get my hands up in his chest to slow him down. Gotta give our QB time. Harper is swatting at my hands like they're horseflies—gigantic, powerful horseflies."

That comment brought a few chuckles. Chop waited for them to subside before continuing. "So, I'm hand fighting with Harper, struggling to keep my hands and arms up into him, but at the same time I am moving my feet too, moving back and to the side. Keeping my balance. Being wary not to step on anybody who might have fallen or gotten knocked down in the backfield. I have to possess great hand and upper-body strength, while displaying the footwork and balance of a ballet dancer. Otherwise, I fall on my booty."

"And that's some serious booty," Marcus Berringer offered from his place next to Alston. More chuckles followed.

Pork Chop steepled his sausage-like fingers and waited. He cleared his throat. "If I may continue now—I am keeping my 'serious booty' low, keeping my leverage on Harper. I push him off, move back, then prepare to battle him again. By now, Hammond shoulda thrown the ball, but he's kept drifting back in the pocket because no one is open. So Harper has one more shot at him. He loads up and tries to charge through me one more time. But he's too desperate, too eager. He's off balance, and I put him on the ground. I pancake the dude. Ah, the pancake block—the offensive lineman's touchdown.

"Meanwhile, Hammond realizes he has taken way too much time, so he—finally—tucks the ball under his arm and sprints left. He picks up twelve yards and a first down. That's just one play for me. All in all, we run sixty offensive plays, thirty-one of 'em passes. I don't allow a single sack all day—and just one 'pressure.' What's most important, I help the O-line make our team goal. Two hundred yards rushing and no sacks. Not a bad day's work for a dumb lineman, huh, Alston?"

Cody studied Alston. He shoulders slumped as he slid forward in his chair. He said nothing. Robyn turned to Pork Chop. "Deke," she said, "you rock. I had no idea how complex you guys have it on the O-line. I'm impressed."

Chop smiled. "It is pretty impressive, isn't it?"

Cody saw Mr. Dellis push himself off his desk. "May we continue now, Mr. Porter?" he asked. Cody was sure the question was meant to be sarcastic, but the teacher's voice sounded quite sincere.

Chop considered the query for a few moments before saying, softly, as he made a sweeping gesture with his right hand, "Be my guest, but the bell rings in less than a minute."

Cody tried to catch up to Robyn when World History ended. But she ignored him, striding toward the exit as if in the middle of a fire drill. Chop clapped him across the back, nearly knocking him off balance. "Let's talk after practice."

After practice was over, Pork Chop and Cody remained on the field. Chop slid his helmet off of his head and turned to face his friend. "You need to feel what I'm about to say, dawg," he said, a hint of sadness in his voice—or was it disappointment?

"Sure, Chop—and thanks for bailing me out in Dellis's class," Cody replied. "What's up?"

Pork Chop pointed to his face. "It would be crazy to try to hide that I'm black, right?"

Cody wrinkled his forehead. "Of course it would, Chop. I mean, why would you want to, anyway? You're proud of who you are."

"That I am. Are you?"

"Am I what?"

"Proud of who you are, what you are?"

Cody held up both hands, as if fending off the block of a hard-charging wide receiver. "Look, it's not that I'm ashamed of my faith or anything. I just don't want to get into it with Dellis, that's all."

Pork Chop started making a robotic, rhythmic beeping sound.

Cody rolled his eyes. "Okay, Chop, what's up with the beeps. Are you impersonating a microwave oven or something?"

"Nope. Beep. Beep. Beep. This is my smoke detector. Beep. Beep. Beep. It tends to go off when somebody blows smoke at me."

Cody exhaled and blinked his eyes. "What—you think I'm lying?"

Pork Chop shrugged. "The smoke detector doesn't lie. Look dawg, I know what it's like to be a minority, especially in this town. You know how many times I sit in a movie theater or restaurant and I'm the only brother in the house? You think that sometimes I don't wish that I could just blend in—avoid the stares, the whispered exchanges?"

"But, Chop, I don't think we're talking about the same thing here."

"It's the same *kind* of thing. I know what some people see when they look at me—a dishonest, profanity-spewin' thug with a chip on his shoulder—and probably a gun tucked in the waistband of his drawers. Hide your money. Hide your women. And I know what some people think when they hear you are a Christian—science-hating, judgmental, hypocritical rightwing fanatic."

Cody considered the comparison. "I never thought of it that way," he said. "You're right. I guess that's one more thing we have in common. But I want you to know—I'm not ashamed of God, but I guess I am afraid of how people will label me because I believe in him. I don't want to be stereotyped. You know what I mean?"

Pork Chop fake coughed. "Are you kiddin' me?"

"But how do you deal with it, Chop? How do you keep from being labeled?"

Cody felt the warmth of his friend's smile. It was a big brother kind of smile. "Code," Chop said, "the labels won't stick to you if you don't let them. And the best way to keep 'em off you is to just be who you be. Don't worry about what people might say or might think. Even what I might think—and you know we don't see eye-to-eye on this particular subject. But still, you gotta—"

"Be who you be," Cody finished the sentence, his voice a guilty half whisper.

The next morning, Cody patted his dad on the back before heading off for school. "Good to see you eating a healthy breakfast, Dad," he said, eyeing his father's bowl of bran flakes. "How are the wedding plans coming along?"

His father looked up from his cereal. "Okay, I guess. You seem in a good mood this morning—hey, what's that you're carrying?"

"It's my study Bible. Gonna do some reading in study hall. And I think I might need it in World History too."

His dad frowned. "But why not take your pocket Bible? It would be a lot easier to carry. And not quite so—uh—conspicuous."

Cody headed for the door. "You know, Dad," he said, smiling. "Sometimes you just gotta be who you be."

In game seven of the season, Grant faced Maranatha. As the bus rumbled to the game, Cody hoped the varsity Eagles would fare as well as the frosh had.

Grant hadn't scored more than thirteen points since the season opener, and the coaching staff had been merciless on the offense ever since. Cody thought they were due for a breakout game, and he was right.

ATV did most of the breaking. He had ninety-nine yards on nine carries at halftime, taking the Eagles to a 14–0 lead.

Phillips scored on an end-around early in the third, and ATV pushed a pile of defenders seven yards on the way to his third TD of the game.

With a 28–0 lead early in the fourth quarter, Coach Morgan sent Cody into the game. Cody's fingers trembled as he tried to fasten his chin strap. He had seen little action since being called up to varsity— just some spot duty against St. Stevens and one series against Mill Creek.

Cody lined up against a towering Crusader end, who looked at least six foot two. On first down, Maranatha ran a quarterback draw. The end threw a vicious block on Cody, knocking him two steps backward, but Cody kept his feet and was ready to lay a hit of his own on his opponent when the referee blew the play dead after a seven-yard gain.

On second down the end came for him again but, instead of laying a block on Cody, hesitated and then streaked down the field. "Pass! Pass!" Cody heard coaches and teammates shouting from the sideline. He sensed where the pass was going: long, and to *his* opponent.

Cody struggled to stay even with the tall receiver, whose long, loping strides gobbled up yards of real estate. Cody tucked close to the receiver's inside shoulder, hoping to keep him breaking toward the middle of the field.

But this was a simple fly pattern. The receiver's goal was simple: outrun Cody and catch the ball.

He did one of the two. But that was enough. McCall, Maranatha's quarterback, hummed a tight spiral that the receiver caught over his outside shoulder as he crossed midfield. Cody stuck to him like Velcro, but the ball was so well thrown that he was helpless to make a play.

He felt anger and panic boiling inside him as his man tried to accelerate and leave him behind. Cody reached with his right hand and grabbed a handful of white jersey, then did the same with his left.

Man, this guy is big, Cody thought, *but if he wants to score, he's gonna have to drag me all the way to the end zone.*

As they crossed the twenty with Cody doing little more than slowing the receiver down, he feared his prediction would come true.

Then Brendan Clark arrived. He hit the receiver so hard that Cody was sent flying. The Maranatha player went down face first at the ten. Clark helped his victim up, and even helped clear away the divot of sod that had lodged in his face mask.

Coach Alvin motioned for Cody to come out of the game. He trotted to the sideline, to where Coaches Alvin and Morgan stood side by side. *You must not cry*, he told himself, *no matter what they call you. Just take it like a man.*

Coach Morgan looked at his assistant and patted Cody on the helmet. "Good coverage, Martin. You stuck right with him. If McCall doesn't throw a perfect pass, that's an incompletion or an I-N-T. Good job. Keep your head up. You'll probably get another series or two before the game is over."

Chapter 7

The
Pain
Pool

Cody survived the rest of the Maranatha game, which Grant won 28–7. ATV gained 208 yards rushing, averaging 9.1 yards a carry. Cody's man caught one more pass on him, this one on a dig-and-go, but Berringer was there to help drag him down after a modest twelve-yard gain.

The win moved Grant's overall record to 4–3, 4–1 in the league. That made the regular-season finale against Claxton Hills crucial. Whoever won that game would move on to the playoffs. The other team was done for the year.

Cody spent his lunch periods the same way as always since joining the varsity—in the weight room watching game tapes. One of the coaches had taped Claxton Hills' 21–0 spanking of Mill Creek.

"Man, those guys look big," Cody whispered to Paul Goddard during Wednesday's video session.

"Yeah," Goddard muttered, with grudging admiration. "Their lines average about 220 pounds. We barely average 200. I don't like those guys. Bunch of rich white boys who think they are living the thug life. Their parents spend about six grand a year in tuition—how ghetto is that?"

Cody cocked his head. "You don't like 'em just because they're rich?"

"No, freshman," came the reply, "I don't like them because they're cocky—and they play dirty. They have pain pools for every game. And they do it differently than other schools. It's not random. They pick one guy to target each game. Rich alumni fund it. Put the target out of the game, not just for a few plays, and you get a hundred bucks or something."

The traditional Thursday dinner was held at Brendan Clark's house that week. A group of parents grilled more than 150 hamburgers and tossed what looked to Cody like a Jacuzzi full of salad. There were no leftovers. After dinner, players dispersed throughout the Clarks' two-story house, some playing video games, others shooting pool in the basement or watching a college football game on ESPN.

Soon, the coaches gathered everyone in the living room for a big-screen TV viewing of *Remember the Titans.*

Last on the Thursday night agenda was the team meeting in the Clarks' three-car garage. After Coaches Morgan, Alvin, and Curtis gave brief speeches, they opened up the floor to the players. Usually, several Eagles took advantage of the opportunity—to thank their coaches, to make commitments regarding the upcoming game, or to challenge or encourage a teammate. Parents, while welcome everywhere else, were barred from these meetings.

ATV spoke first, promising his teammates that he would run harder than ever the following evening. Tucker challenged defense to put pressure on Claxton Hills' six-four QB Eric Faust. And he thanked Brendan Clark, whom he called "the best teammate I could ever hope to have."

That set the stage for Clark. "Seniors, this could be our last game," he began slowly. "Or at least our last game in front of our home crowd. Let's give everyone something to remember. I promise to play the game of my life. I owe each of you that—my teammates, my coaches."

Clark paused. Cody wondered if he had forgotten what he wanted to say next, but when he began to speak again, his voice was trembling. "And let's make our parents proud too. Some of you might know that my mom and dad separated over the summer. But they're both here tonight, and they'll both be there tomorrow. I can't help but think that if I have a special game, it will, you know, help them somehow."

Coach Morgan moved to Clark's side, put his arm around him, and led him to the back of the garage. Cody could see the linebacker's massive shoulders heaving. Cody swallowed hard. "And some people say this is just a game," he whispered.

A few high gray clouds dotted the sky above Grant Field. Cody stood on the sideline with his varsity teammates and watched the seemingly endless stream of headlights approach the stadium. The home bleachers were already almost full; the latecomers would have to stand along the chain-link fence around the field, sit behind the end zones, or view the game from their cars.

Presently, Cody heard the voice of the public address announcer: "Welcome to Senior Night at Grant Field, for the final regular-season contest of the year. Please direct your attention to the center of the field, as we honor our Grant Eagle seniors and their parents."

Cody felt the back of his neck tingle as Brendan Clark's name was announced. The linebacker took a rose from a cheerleader, then jogged to midfield, where his mother and father waited, the former wearing a number 51 game jersey just like her son's. She used one of the too-long sleeves to dab at her eyes while Clark gave his father a fierce hug. Then he kissed his mother on the forehead, hugged her carefully, and stood proudly beside his parents.

Cody noticed that a few of the seniors, including ATV, exchanged awkward handshakes rather than hugs with their dads. He wondered which it would be when he was a senior. And he wondered if Beth would be there at midfield. Then he remembered something he had read in his giant study Bible only two days ago. "Each day has enough trouble of its own."

Yeah, he thought grimly, *ain't that the truth?*

ATV smacked the opening kick off the left upright of the opposing end zone. Coach Morgan began the game with three defensive backs, but it became clear that Claxton Hills planned to fill the late-October air with flying footballs. Eric Faust guided the Lancers to the Grant twenty-eight before a sack by Tucker moved them out of field-goal range.

Grant went nowhere on its first possession, and Morgan gambled one more time with his three-DB scheme. Faust made him pay, completing seven of nine passes for fifty-eight yards as Claxton Hills hushed the home field with an effective TD drive.

"Martin," Coach Alvin snapped, after a turnover gave the Lancers the ball again. "over here, pronto!"

Cody knew what was coming. "Look," the coach said, his eyes wide, "you're going in. Faust is killing us out there. It's time for you to earn your spurs. You hear?"

Cody nodded.

Coach Alvin grabbed his face mask and pulled him close. "Don't get nervous out there. You play the game. Play smart. Don't let 'em intimidate you."

Cody nodded again. He wasn't sure if he could speak, so he deemed it best not to risk it.

Cody could swear that Butler, rather stocky for a wideout, was sneering at him as they faced off on first down. Butler ran a down-and-out, with Cody shadowing him. As Butler made his cut, he used his left hand to push Cody in the chest, creating space between them. Faust's throw hit the turf or the Lancers would have picked up a first down.

"You're lucky, boy," Butler snarled as they jogged back to the line of scrimmage.

Faust threw to the other side of the field on their next two plays, both incompletions.

Cody jogged to the sideline, almost limp from relief. *What I could use now*, he thought, *is a nice long drive from our offense, preferably one that takes us right up to halftime.*

Grant did move the ball well on its next possession. The Lancers five down-linemen stood almost shoe to shoe, with their three linebackers tucked in right behind them—daring ATV to try to gain ground up the middle.

Unfortunately for the visitors, they had apparently forgotten about ATV's 4.7 speed. On first down, he took a pitch from Hammond and romped around the right end for twenty-eight yards. Next, Hammond faked a handoff to ATV, then scooted around the left end for another twenty-four.

Despite their larger size, the Lancers were back on their heels. Pork Chop and the rest of the offensive linemen fired off the ball in unison, moving like a blue-and-silver wave. And once they made contact with the defense, they held their blocks, allowing the Eagle backs to make cuts toward the open portions of the field.

ATV finished the clock-devouring drive with a one-yard plunge right into the teeth of the Claxton Hills defense.

On the next defensive series, Cody absorbed three vicious blocks from Butler, but no passes came his way.

On Claxton Hills' final drive of the first half, Butler beat Cody on a shallow slant route, but Clark was there to mop up. He hit Butler so hard that at first Cody thought he had injured himself.

Cody felt panic wash over him as he watched Clark jog to the sideline pointing at his chest.

The linebacker joined the defensive huddle two plays later. "Are you okay?" Cody asked him.

Clark exchanged a knowing smile with Tucker. "Of course I am. Just hit Butler so hard I snapped the laces on my shoulder pads."

"Oh, no, not again, Brendan," Tucker mock-scolded him. "You know how expensive those laces are."

The Lancers missed a forty-two-yard field goal to end the half, and the teams trotted to their respective locker rooms with the game knotted at seven-all.

Coach Morgan outlined some defensive adjustments. Then he gave his players a few minutes to gather themselves.

Cody sat between Pork Chop and Marcus Berringer on a narrow wooden bench. He looked around the locker room. Grass and chunks of mud, dropped from players' cleats, littered the floor. Cody stared at his battered locker. Several dents and dings framed it, as if someone had attacked it with a hammer. Then, near the center, it was marked by a serious crater—it had to be the result of a helmet. All season he wondered if the helmet had a head in it at the time.

He looked across the locker room. ATV was lying on his back on a bench, bloody knuckles folded across his chest. He was listening to his MP3 player, no doubt some pounding hard rock, in an effort to psych himself up for the second half. Sweat pooled on the floor beneath him. Cody knew ATV had to be close to one hundred yards rushing already—against a defense custom-designed to stop him.

Pork Chop rose wearily from the bench next to Cody and walked to the entrance, where Vance, the trainer, not the coach, was summoning him.

He returned a few moments later, eyes grim. "Dawg," he said. "I have bad news for you."

Cody let out a moan. "What now?"

"I just heard—you're the pain pool target this game."

Cody shook his head in disbelief. "I don't get it. Me? I play defense. I'm the smallest guy on the team."

Pork Chop nodded. "There you go. A little freshman playing varsity. The perfect target."

Cody felt fear rising in him like smoke. "What do I do, Chop?" he asked, hoping his friend couldn't hear the terror in his voice.

"You watch your back, my brother. I'll be watching it too. And I'll tell Coach M and the guys. One more thing—if I were you, I'd pray."

Cody smiled a sad smile. "Already did that."

Pork Chop patted him on the shoulder blade. "I should have known."

"Hey, Chop," Cody asked, cocking his head. "how did you find this out?"

Chop smiled. "Robyn heard it in line at the concession stand. She went to Vance right away. By the way, she has two messages for you: First, she says she's praying for you. Second, she said to tell you she really likes your Bible."

Well, thought Cody as he slid his shoulder pads back on, *sounds like I'm off Robyn's hit list. Too bad I'm still on Claxton Hills'. But at least now I know why Butler has been charging at me like a rhino all night.*

Grant received the second-half kickoff and mounted an ugly but effective drive. It was ATV up the middle, ATV off left tackle, ATV off right tackle, and ATV on screen passes. Hammond threw in a couple of QB keepers just to keep the defense honest, but 99 percent of the time, they knew what was coming.

Coach Alvin paced the sideline like a guard dog, sometimes losing control and marching ten yards onto the field to protest a call or scream at a blocker. But most of the time he was intent on keeping ATV motivated. "Just keep running at 'em, big man—they can't stop you!" he shouted, his voice ragged. "All you gotta do is pick up 3.3 yards a carry, and the first-down chains keep movin'!"

"Amen to that," Cody whispered.

ATV's workhorse efforts eventually brought the Eagles a first down at the Lancer fourteen. That's when Hammond decided to change things up and put the ball in the air—right to Hayden Owens-Tharpe, an all-conference cornerback and wide receiver. Owens-Tharpe made the pick in the left corner of the end zone and ran it out to the twelve.

Cody ran onto the field with the defense. He stood facing Butler, the wind whistling through his ear holes. He wondered if he could stay out of the pain pool.

Claxton Hills ran a QB sweep on first down, trying to take advantage of Faust's size and decent speed. The run went to the opposite side of the field from Cody, but he pursued the play, just in case Faust got around the end or cut back to the middle. Tucker contained the play, turning Faust right into Goddard, who wrapped the QB up. Faust kept his legs pumping, but all that did was give time for Clark to come flying in. He knocked both Faust and Goddard to the ground.

While Cody stood marveling at the double tackle, Owens-Tharpe blindsided him with a helmet-to-helmet hit that knocked him sideways. He fought to keep his feet, but the momentum was too great. He tumbled to the turf, pain exploding like a cherry bomb in his head. *So much for staying out of the pain pool*, he thought.

His friend nodded. "I think we need a fourth DB. And besides, if you go back in the game, Owens-Jerk—I mean Tharpe—doesn't get the pain-pool money."

Cody exchanged fist pounds with Chop, then snapped his chin strap. He ran to Coach Morgan. "Put me in," he said.

Cody never thought he had the spiritual gift of prophecy, but as he stood in the defensive backfield, paired against Butler again, he knew the play was coming his way. He also knew Butler would need to catch a pass along the sideline. The Lancers had only one time-out remaining, and they would want to save that to get their field goal team on the field if they had the chance.

As Faust barked out the snap count, Cody edged a bit toward the sideline, hoping to tempt Butler to take the inside leverage. He eyed the first-down marker. The pass pattern, whatever it was, would have to get to that point.

Butler exploded off the line on the snap of the ball. He chugged toward Cody, giving a fake to the inside of the field, a fake Cody ignored.

Yeah, right, he thought as he raced Butler to the sideline.

Faust must have seen that Cody had the outside position on Butler because he threw the ball low and slightly behind his receiver, hoping that he could come back for it and make a diving catch.

Butler, seemingly reading his QB's mind, dug his cleats into the turf, turned, and lunged for the ball.

The pass was too low and too hard. It hit the turf before Butler could pull it in. Cody felt someone fly by him on his outside shoulder. It was Berringer, coming up from his safety position to make the play. Seeing that Butler was already down, he tried to hurdle him.

Unfortunately for the Lancer wideout, Berringer didn't have much hurdling experience. His left cleat landed squarely on Butler's right hand. Cody heard his opponent cry out in pain.

The incompletion brought up fourth down. Claxton Hills would have to go for it. They weren't in field goal range, and if they punted the ball back to Grant, the Eagles could run out the clock. Cody paused a moment before joining the defensive huddle. He watched Butler, holding his right hand in his left, head for the offensive huddle.

"Okay, guys," Clark told his teammates. "Listen up. This could be the season right here. It's gonna be a pass. Be ready. I'm blitzin' like a mad dog."

"Me too," Cody said, surprised by his own words.

Clark looked at him. "Code—you sure?"

Cody nodded. "Butler's hand is messed up. There's no way they'll throw to him. He's just a decoy. If you blitz, they'll all pay attention to you. I'll have a clean shot."

Clark looked at him and nodded. Tucker rubbed his hands together excitedly. "Hit him hard, man!" he urged. "Hit him real hard!"

Butler rested his injured hand on his thigh pad as he waited on the snap count. Cody thought about what Clark had said the night before, about wanting to win for his parents. He thought of all the seniors and how they wanted this to be a game they would remember. Then he launched himself at Faust.

The Lancer QB was looking for Owens-Tharpe over the middle. The fullback, the only protection in the backfield, was helping the center and left guard triple-team a snarling, charging Brendan Clark.

Faust cocked the ball behind his ear just as Cody closed in on him. Cody lunged at the passing arm; he knew he would probably just bounce off if he tried to hit the QB in his torso. He leaped on the arm as if it were a low-hanging tree branch, his weight pulling Faust off balance. Cody saw the ball squirt free.

As soon as he hit the turf, he bounced right back up and scrambled for the ball. Slowing only slightly, he scooped the pigskin into his arms at the Grant forty-five. The goal line was fifty-five yards away.

Cody exploded across midfield, eyes cast slightly downward. Under his feet, the field was a blur of green grass and white hash marks.

He felt he was running from not just the Lancers he felt pursuing him from behind, but from the ghost of Gabe Weitz, the pain of losing his mom, and the fear of his dad having a new wife. He vowed that he was going to outrun them all. He crossed the thirty, then the twenty. Out of the corner of his eye, he saw Owens-Tharpe angling toward him. It was going to be close.

At the ten, Cody knew there was going to be contact. The Lancer receiver hurled himself with an animal growl.

The growl told Cody that his would-be tackler was desperate—and probably angry about losing out on the pain pool. It told him that Owens-Tharpe would be head-hunting. It told him to duck.

Cody dipped his head and torso as if he were running through a tunnel. Owens-Tharpe flew over the top of him—delivering only a glancing blow to his helmet—and landed on the orange pylon in the near corner of the end zone.

Cody absorbed the hit, placing his hand on the turf to keep his balance. He saw the goal line and dove across it. He stood and looked to the home bleachers.

The Grant fans were screaming, jumping up and down, and banging ThunderStix. He saw his dad and Beth jumping up and down in near-perfect unison. Presently, Brendan Clark sprinted toward him and hoisted him in the air. "What a rush!" he screamed at Cody. "What a rush!"

When Clark deposited him back on the field, Cody handed him the football. "This is for you, Brendan. And for your mom and dad too. God bless."

Clark took off his helmet. And then, for the first time in his football career, he kneeled in the end zone and prayed. Cody hesitated for a moment, then joined him.

Epilogue

After Cody's game-breaking play, he knew the Lancers were still clinging to the hope of a last-ditch miracle of their own. Once ATV booted the ball into the stratosphere, they would have over a minute to move the ball eighty yards, with one time-out still on the clock. It was a formidable challenge but not impossible.

ATV teed the ball up, moved back into position, then rumbled toward the ball. *I wonder how far this one's gonna go*, Cody wondered.

As it turned out, about fifteen yards. ATV executed a textbook onside kick, the ball dribbling close to the ground. The Lancers were caught off guard. Clark pounced on the ball, and it was game over.

As the Eagles trudged up to the locker room toward what was sure to be one of the most raucous celebrations in school history, Clark drew alongside Cody.

"So, Martin," he said, "praying in the end zone. I thought that kinda thing wasn't your bag?"

Cody smiled. "Maybe not always," he answered, "but as the wise philosopher Pork Chop Porter once said, 'Sometimes you gotta be who you be.'"

Chapter 1
Unfinished Business

Cody Martin smiled as he walked past the Grant High School gym. *Ah, the sights and sounds of basketball practice,* he thought. *You gotta love 'em.*

He stopped momentarily at the south gym doorway and surveyed the flurry of activity: the rat-a-tat slapping of leather on hardwood as Terry Alston showed off his dribbling skills near the south baseline. The clang of Greg "the Cannon" Gannon's high-arcing jump shots as he tried to find his range from twenty feet. The squeaking of Terrance Dylan's shoes as he ran agility drills along the east sideline. Taking stock of it all was Coach Clayton, who had moved up from his Grant

Middle School position to lead the Eagle freshmen. The loose-limbed coach prowled the near sideline sporting a brand-new blue and silver warm-up suit, offering such helpful pointers as, "For the love of Rick Barry, will you puh-leeze concentrate when you shoot free throws, Mr. Matt Slaven?"

It was 6:25 in the morning on the second Monday of November, five minutes before the first frosh basketball practice. Gannon launched an air ball and almost ran into Cody as he scrambled to retrieve it.

"Hey, Martin," he panted. "You gonna join us this morning?"

Cody wagged his head. "Uh, Gannon, it's still football season for me. Second round of the play-offs are this Friday, in case you haven't heard."

Gannon shrugged. "I know. I just thought you might put in double duty. You know, run with us in the mornings, do football in the afternoons."

"Did a basketball hit you in the head, dude?" Cody asked with a chuckle. "I'm so sore I'm walking like Frankenstein. That's why I'm here so early. Gonna take a whirlpool, gonna have Dutch help me with some stretching."

"Well, I wish you guys well," Gannon said. "But we're gonna miss you. And Pork Chop, too. It rocks that you're both playing varsity football as freshmen. But we're thin without you. Especially on defense. We need some stoppers like you and the big fella. What's Porter weighing now, anyway? About 225? We could use that beef under the boards."

Cody turned to the locker room. "Hey, I hope we're out here with you soon," he said. "But not *too* soon."

With an involuntary groan, Cody slowly lowered himself into the bubbling water of the stainless steel whirlpool tub in the training room. *I wonder if there's any part of me that* doesn't *hurt.* He considered the question for a moment. *Maybe my hair. And I think my ears are okay.*

As he felt his aching muscles begin to relax, he leaned his head back and replayed the highlights of the Grant Eagles' win in the opening round of the Colorado high school football play-offs, just two days before.

Bishop Moreland was a Catholic school in the southern part of the state. Cody and his teammates had watched a videotape on them during their lunch hours leading up to the game. The Bulldogs were huge, but they looked a bit slow. Their offensive line didn't explode off the snap the way Pork Chop and his O-line teammates did.

On the other hand, Moreland had a 230-pound fullback named Michaels who played like a human

Neither team was able to generate much offense in the third quarter. Bryce Phillips, the Eagles' best wideout, picked up fifteen yards on an end-around, but as he struggled to churn out a few extra yards, he fumbled near midfield, halting Grant's only promising drive of the quarter.

The Bulldogs took over and, for the first time in the game, sent in two wideouts. "Okay," Coach Curtis barked. "Standard defense in—now! Two safeties, two corners!"

Cody swallowed hard as he buckled his chin strap and slid in his teeth guard.

He lined up at cornerback against number 84, a lanky wide receiver on the weak side (opposite the tight end) of the Bulldog line. As the center hiked the ball, the receiver charged at Cody, growling and snarling like an angry beast.

Cody held his ground, sending 84 a telepathic message: *All that noise might have worked against me early in the season, dude. But since then I've been growled at, screamed at, cussed at, and threatened by all kinds of guys bigger than me. So you're gonna have to bring something more than noise.*

Cody raised his arms and chucked 84 hard across the shoulder pads, then stepped inside him as he saw Michaels slide off-tackle and rumble upfield. Clark

zonder**kidz**.

We want to hear from you. Please send your comments
about this book to us in care of zreview@zondervan.com. Thank you.

Grand Rapids, MI 49530
www.zonderkidz.com